MY FAVORITE MISTAKE

Also by Georgina Bloomberg
& Catherine Hapka

The A Circuit

MY FAVORITE MISTAKE

AN A CIRCUIT NOVEL

GEORGINA BLOOMBERG
& CATHERINE HAPKA

BLOOMSBURY

NEW YORK BERLIN LONDON SYDNEY

First published in the United States of America in March 2012
by Bloomsbury Books for Young Readers
www.bloomsburyteens.com

For information about permission to reproduce selections from this book, write to
Permissions, Bloomsbury BFYR, 175 Fifth Avenue, New York, New York 10010

Library of Congress Cataloging-in-Publication Data
Bloomberg, Georgina.
My favorite mistake : an A circuit novel /
by Georgina Bloomberg and Catherine Hapka. — 1st U.S. ed.
p.   cm.
Summary: Teen equestrians Tommi, Kate, and Zara try to put aside thoughts of boyfriends and
family issues as they continue to compete on the elite A-circuit, but secrets they are keeping
from one another prove more problematic.
ISBN 978-1-59990-755-0 (hardcover) • ISBN 978-1-59990-642-3 (paperback)
[1. Horse shows—Fiction.   2. Horsemanship—Fiction.   3. Friendship—Fiction.
4. Wealth—Fiction.   5. New York (N.Y.)—Fiction.]   I. Hapka, Catherine.   II. Title.
PZ7.B62345My 2012   [Fic]—dc23   2011015083

Book design by Regina Roff
Typeset by Westchester Book Composition
Printed in the U.S.A. by Quad/Graphics, Fairfield, Pennsylvania
2 4 6 8 10 9 7 5 3 1 (hardcover)
2 4 6 8 10 9 7 5 3 1 (paperback)

To my father, Michael. Thank you for showing me that
nothing is out of reach if you believe in yourself.
—G. B.

ONE

▬ ▬ ▬ ▬ ▬

Tommi wandered toward the floor-to-ceiling wall of windows, ignoring the sounds of the party going on behind her. Her friend Courtney's penthouse apartment was right on Central Park South, and even though Tommi had been there many times, she never got tired of looking out over the park.

"Nice view, huh?" someone said from behind her.

She glanced back. The guy standing there was named Alex Nakano, and Tommi had only met him an hour ago. But she was already intrigued. For one thing, he was hot with a capital wow. He'd told her that his father was a Japanese-American hedge fund manager and his mother a Brazilian-born art dealer with an exclusive little gallery space down in SoHo. Alex's multi-culti heritage had combined to give him a totally unique look—spiky dark hair, toffee-colored eyes, a lean, compact body—plus a mischievous little smirk that seemed to be all his own. It had been a long time since Tommi had felt such an immediate spark with anyone, and she was enjoying the feeling.

"Yeah," she said with a smile. "That's one thing you don't get in a brownstone. All I can see from my room is the house across the street."

"Yo, turn the music down!" a girl shouted from the other end of the room. "My parents will totally lose it if they find out I had a party."

"Shoulda thought of that before you invited us, Court!" a skinny guy with freckles called out. Duckface. One of Tommi's oldest friends. With a shout of laughter, he jumped onto the baby grand and started doing the chicken dance.

Alex grinned, raising his beer and hooting along with most of the other partiers. Then he turned back to Tommi.

"It's not really a party unless Duckface is there, is it?" he said.

Tommi laughed. "Words to live by." She watched with amusement as Duckface switched to the cancan, almost falling off the piano.

When a couple of friends dragged him down and over toward the bar, Tommi turned to face the window again. The wooded expanse of the park looked mysterious and dark amid the lights and high-rises of the city surrounding it.

"Seriously, though," Tommi said, the gin and tonic she'd had earlier in the evening making her feel relaxed and pensive. "I love Manhattan, but it must be nice sometimes—living where you do out in the Hamptons. Or anywhere like that, you know?" She shot Alex a look. "Maybe someday I'll have the best of both worlds. A nice place in the city so I can still go out and have fun, plus a few acres out in the country somewhere for when I need to relax."

"With a few horses out back, maybe?" Alex asked.

Tommi had learned long ago that there were exactly two things that everyone in the world seemed to know about her. One was that her father was Richard Aaronson, the super-genius Wall Street billionaire. The other was that she spent most of her free time riding horses.

"Maybe," she said. "It's kind of hard to imagine my horses living anywhere but Pelham Lane, though. So maybe I'll just buy the place next door. That way I can walk over any time I want, but my horses get to keep living in the style they've become accustomed to."

"Pelham Lane?"

"Pelham Lane Stables. My barn," Tommi explained. "My trainer's barn, I mean. I ride with Jamie Vos."

"Oh," Alex said politely.

Tommi laughed. "Sorry, I always forget that non-horse people mostly don't even know who he is. It's kind of weird to realize that, actually, since in the riding world he's a total rock star."

"Really? So you're saying this guy is like the Vince Lombardi of jumping horses over stuff?"

"Yeah, pretty much. He's an amazing rider and trainer. We go to all the big A shows, and to Florida in the winter. It's awesome."

This was usually about the point when people started to zone out and look bored, no matter how polite they were trying to be. And that was okay. Sure, Tommi was pretty much obsessed with riding and showing. That didn't mean she couldn't talk about anything else.

But before she could change the subject to music or movies or something, Alex leaned a little closer. "So how long have you been riding there?" he asked.

She was surprised to see that he actually looked interested. "Practically forever," she said. "My older sister started taking lessons there first. One day I tagged along, and the rest is history."

After that Alex kept asking questions, and Tommi kept answering them. It was kind of a novelty talking so much to a guy about riding. Her last boyfriend had pretended to snore every time she even approached the subject. Yeah, he'd thought that was really funny. One of the many reasons they'd broken up right after their school's prom a few months earlier.

Tommi was trying to explain the difference between hunters and jumpers when Courtney's boyfriend, Parker, wandered over. He was tall and skinny, with a mop of blond hair and perpetually rosy cheeks that made him look closer to seven than seventeen.

"What a surprise," he said with a smirk. "Tommi's blabbing about horsies."

Tommi rolled her eyes. "For your information, some people are actually interested in other people's lives, Parker," she said with a matching smirk. "Not everyone is totally self-absorbed like you."

"Yeah, it's cool," Alex put in. "I love talking to anyone who's really passionate about something, you know?"

"Whatever, dude." Parker grinned at them both. "I had a feeling you guys might hit it off. Woulda introduced you sooner, except Court thought you and Grant—well, you know." He raised an eyebrow at Tommi, then shot a glance at a handsome, broad-shouldered, preppy-looking guy chatting with a couple of people halfway across the room.

Okay, awkward. "Yeah," Tommi said quickly. "Um, so you guys are neighbors out in the Hamptons, huh?"

"Uh-huh," Alex said. "My bedroom window looks right over their tennis courts."

"Right." Parker puffed out his skinny chest. "So he knew the first day he moved in that I'm a tennis superstud."

Alex laughed. "More like I knew right away you can't play for crap."

"Maybe true," Parker retorted. "But I can still whip your ass in straight sets."

As the two guys continued to razz each other, Tommi sneaked another peek at Grant. She'd known him since they were little kids, though they'd kind of lost touch when he moved to Europe for a couple of years. When he'd returned earlier this summer, taller and handsomer and much more self-assured, Tommi had actually wondered if it was time to turn their lifelong friendship into something more.

But no. She'd quickly realized that while Grant was an amazing guy, there was just no romantic spark there. At least not on her side. He seemed to feel different, and she'd had to let him down easy after he came to watch her ride at the big Hounds Hollow show the previous weekend.

It was definitely a little awkward being at this party with him, flirting with another guy right under his nose. But Grant didn't seem bothered by it—in fact, he didn't even seem to notice. So Tommi tried not to worry about it.

— 5 —

She checked her watch. "Oops, I should probably go," she said, breaking into Parker's bragging about his backhand or whatever. "It's getting late."

"What? No way!" Alex protested. "It's still early."

Parker grinned. "Yeah. Anyone who leaves before two gets the loser award."

"Guess I'll have to live with the shame." Tommi started looking around for her purse. "Because I told my trainer I'd be at the barn early tomorrow."

"So what?" Alex shrugged. "It sounds like you're the barn's superstar rider. He'll get over it if you blow him off this one time, right?"

Tommi knew she had to cut Alex some slack. He couldn't be expected to know that you just didn't blow off Jamie Vos, no matter how much money your father had or how many ribbons you'd won. No way. Jamie might seem mild-mannered and friendly on the surface, but he hadn't become one of the most successful trainers on the circuit by being a pushover.

Besides, in this case Jamie was doing her a favor. He'd offered to come down to the barn an hour before his first lesson of the day so he could watch her ride Legs, her new investment horse, and give her some tips.

"Seriously, I wish I could stay," she said. "But it's hard to ride well when you're falling asleep in the saddle."

"Come on, just stay a little bit longer," Alex wheedled, grabbing her hand.

"Yeah, live a little, Tommi," Parker put in. "You can sleep when you're dead."

"I *will* be dead if I'm late tomorrow." Tommi was distracted by the feeling of Alex's hand squeezing hers. Not to mention the way he was looking at her with big puppy-dog eyes—as if her decision to stay or go would make or break his whole night.

Besides, he was right. They both were. What could it hurt to stay a little longer? All she'd lose was some sleep. No big deal.

"Maybe half an hour," she relented. "But then I've really got to go."

Alex grinned. "Cool. I'll take what I can get."

Just then Duckface came dancing over, three or four giggling girls following him in a sloppy conga line. Duckface waved his Corona over his head in salute to the group by the window. "We should do this way more often, you guys," he said, his words slightly slurred. "Like, every weekend."

"Yeah," one of the giggling girls put in. "Court, you should totally convince your parents to go to Bermuda all the time."

Courtney, who'd just wandered over to check her magenta-streaked blond hair in the reflective surface of the window, rolled her eyes. "Right," she said. "This is the last time I let any of you idiots near my house."

Parker grinned and kissed her on the top of her head. "We'll see about that."

"I've got an idea," Alex spoke up. "How about a house party out at my place? My folks are in Brazil all month—if I bribe the house manager, he'll totally let you all crash there for a few days."

"Seriously?" Duckface said. "I'm so there, dude!"

"Me too." Parker glanced around at the others. "You guys should see Nakano's place. The pool's amazing."

"A pool? Count me in!" one of the girls said eagerly.

"Sweet," Alex said. "We could do it this coming week if you want. My aunt's there this weekend, but she'll be cleared out by Monday afternoon. You guys could come then and stay through Saturday." He grinned and glanced at Courtney. "That'll still give me plenty of time to clean up all the broken stuff before the 'rents get back."

"See?" Parker tapped Courtney on the forehead. "That's planning, my dear."

Courtney just rolled her eyes. Meanwhile Alex turned toward Tommi.

"How about it?" he said. "You were just saying you like to get out of Manhattan sometimes, right?"

"Yeah," Tommi said slowly. "And wow, it sounds great—I really wish I could join you all. But—"

"No buts!" Alex broke in. "You've got to come."

"Like I said, I wish I could. But I've got a show next week, and I'm supposed to drive down there on Tuesday."

Duckface snorted. "Don't be so uptight, Tommi," he said. "It's worth skipping one of your pony rides for a totally epic Hamptons house party."

"Yeah," Alex said. "It won't be the same without you."

His eyes gazed into hers hopefully. She hesitated, trying to figure out how to explain it to him. This wasn't just another horse show—not now that she had Legs to worry about. She'd bought the horse in partnership with her father, and part of the deal was that she had to get him sold by the fall. That meant every show counted right now. She couldn't afford to skip one.

Or could she? Looking into Alex's eyes, she had to wonder.

Sure, riding and showing was important. But so was the rest of her life. Besides, she'd been pushing Legs—and herself—pretty hard. They could both probably use a little time off, right?

"Okay, I definitely can't totally skip the show," she said. "But maybe I can take a pass on the schooling class I was going to do on Wednesday morning. That way I wouldn't need to get there until Thursday. So at least I could sneak out to the Hamptons for a couple of days."

"So you're in?" Alex sounded so psyched that the second thoughts Tommi was already having dissipated instantly. "Cool! It'll be so worth it—we're going to have a blast."

"Yeah." Tommi returned his smile. "I'm sure it'll be worth it."

"Hey, boy. How're you feeling?" Kate Nilsen stepped toward the tall chestnut gelding looking out over his stall guard. The horse leaned forward as she approached, quickly lipping up the carrot chunk she pulled out of her jeans pocket. Just as quickly, he swung his head around, pricking his ears at a cat dashing down the aisle.

Kate felt her stomach clench with anxiety as she watched him. Ford, as the horse was known, had been one of the most promising young show hunters at Pelham Lane.

Now? He was pretty much a useless pasture ornament. At least until he healed from his injuries—if he ever did.

Hearing footsteps, Kate glanced over her shoulder. Marissa, one of the other junior riders at the barn, was walking toward her. "Hi," Marissa said. "How's he doing?"

"He's not happy being stuck in his stall." Kate dodged the horse's big head as he swung around to stare at a bird that had just landed on a nearby windowsill. "Vet says we can hand walk him a little, though. Maybe that will help. I was thinking I might take him out now, actually."

"Cool. Let me know if I can, you know, help or whatever." Marissa's smile looked forced and kind of guilty.

Kate understood, because she shared the same guilt. They'd both witnessed the accident that had robbed this horse of his soundness. So had most of the other junior riders at Pelham Lane. It had happened last weekend at the big Hounds Hollow show. There had been an after-hours party, and a bunch of drunken juniors had decided to play high jumper with some of the Pelham Lane horses. One of those juniors, a new girl named Zara, had ended up flipping Ford over the jump. She'd escaped without injury, but the gelding had pulled a suspensory and fractured his withers.

"I still can't believe we have to lie to Jamie about what happened," Marissa whispered after taking a careful look around to make sure nobody was close enough to hear.

Kate knew what she meant, and then some. It was hard for any of them to lie to Jamie. But it was even worse for Kate. She owed Jamie so much more than the others. If he hadn't agreed to take her on as a working student, she'd still be stuck at her old lesson barn riding half-broke pukes from the local auction. She'd still be dreaming about riding nice horses at the big shows, not doing it.

Yes, she owed him everything. At least everything important. Normally she'd never lie to him. But this wasn't a normal situation. Not even close.

"It sucks," she said softly. "But what can we do? We just have to . . ."

She let her voice trail off as she heard voices at the end of the aisle. A second later several chattering preteens rounded the corner, dressed for their morning lesson. At the same time one of the grooms, a guy in his early twenties named Max, appeared at the other end leading a freshly bathed pony. Even at this early hour on a Sunday morning, the barn was busy. Everyone, from the school kids to the working adults, wanted to get in some riding time before next week's show.

Marissa moved on toward her horse's stall, and Kate gave Ford another pat. "Back in a sec, big guy," she told him. "Just need to grab a lead shank."

She hurried toward the tack room. Spacious and well organized, it was the center of the barn both literally and figuratively. The big bandage trunk in the middle of the room often served double duty as a table, and at the moment bridle parts were scattered across its weathered wooden top—reins, nosebands, and more, all jumbled together. A browband and a couple of curb chains had fallen on the floor, where an elderly bulldog was snuffling at them with his pushed-in nose.

The guy bent over the pile of bits didn't seem to notice. He was scrubbing at some green horse slobber that had dried in the links of a Waterford bit when Kate entered, but looked up immediately when she said his name, flipping back his shock of reddish-blond hair.

"Hey, gorgeous," he greeted her with a rakish smile. Tossing aside the half-cleaned bit, he unfolded his tall, lanky body from its seat on an overturned bucket. In two quick steps he was across the room and giving her a kiss.

"You're here early," she said, a little breathless. Kissing Fitz had that effect on her. Made her forget about everything else, even breathing.

"Tell me about it." Fitz snorted. "Jamie wanted me here at the butt-crack of dawn so I could scrub down his grody tack."

Kate giggled. "Come on. To most people, eight a.m. isn't exactly the butt-crack of dawn."

"Maybe not. But I'm not used to getting up before noon." He leaned in for another kiss. "Now I'm glad I did, though."

Kate only hesitated for a moment before letting go, allowing her body to melt into his. Even after everything that had happened, it still felt really nice to be close to him.

Finally, remembering where they were, she pulled her lips away from his. "We should stop," she whispered. "Someone will see."

"So what? You ashamed of me?" He ran his hands up and down her bare arms. "Not that I'd blame you—I'm totally the barn loser right now." He grinned, actually seeming kind of proud of the fact.

Kate didn't get that. If she was in as much trouble as Fitz was right now, she'd probably be wearing a bag over her head.

"You're on probation, remember?" she said, pulling away and hurrying over to grab a lead shank. "Jamie will freak if he catches you goofing off."

Fitz just shrugged, not looking worried at all. Typical. Fitz wasn't the type to worry about much of anything. And why should he? His family was loaded, and his own quick wit, easy charm, and lanky good looks meant he could have pretty much any girl he wanted. He'd taken full advantage of that, turning playerism into an art form all over the show circuit and beyond.

But things were different with Kate. She hadn't believed that at first, but now she did. What he'd done after Hounds Hollow had pretty much proved it.

"Nobody's here to see us except old Chaucer." Fitz bent down to pat the bulldog, who'd wandered over to drool on Kate's paddock boots. "Can't I get just one more kiss? Come on—even prisoners at Sing Sing get a conjugal visit once in a while."

He grabbed Kate's hand, pulling her closer again. "Well, okay, I guess," she mumbled as his lips found hers again. "But just a quick one . . ."

This time Kate couldn't quite relax into the kiss. Thinking about what had happened last weekend was just another reminder of how different their lives were. When Fitz screwed up, his parents could almost always throw enough money at the situation to make it right again. Kate knew she didn't have that kind of margin of error. Her father's salary as a local cop had barely covered the purchase price of her beater car—no way could he afford to buy her even one hoof of any of the horses at Pelham Lane. Or be able to understand how an animal could cost more than their family home.

Just then someone else burst into the tack room, moving fast. Kate jumped away from Fitz in a panic, then slumped with relief when she saw that it was only Tommi.

"Hi," she said, feeling self-conscious as Tommi's cool brown eyes took in the situation with a faint smile. Kate knew that her friend hadn't approved of her and Fitz getting together at first—Tommi wasn't the type to keep her opinions to herself, and had pretty much come right out and said so. But she seemed to be coming around now. "Did you already finish your ride with Jamie?" Kate asked her.

"Nope, had to postpone—one of the adults wanted to sneak in a lesson before she left on some trip for work or something, so Jamie had to take her first." Tommi stepped over and grabbed her well-broken-in County saddle from its rack. "I'm supposed to meet him in the ring in like twenty minutes."

Kate just nodded. "I'll help you tack up," she said, both disappointed and relieved to have an excuse to escape from Fitz. "See you," she told him without quite meeting his eye. Then she grabbed Tommi's bridle off its hook and hurried out of the room.

Zara was in a pretty good mood as she skipped down the wire-and-wood staircase in her family's spacious SoHo loft.

"Yo, where's Mickey?" she called out to the various people milling around in the big main room below.

A nerdy-looking guy with wire-rimmed glasses—Zara couldn't remember his name, but she was pretty sure he was one of her father's accountants—heard her and glanced up from his laptop. "He's out."

"What? When's he coming back? I need a ride to the barn."

Nerdy Accountant Dude just shrugged, his attention already back on his spreadsheets or whatever. Real helpful. Zara stomped over to the foyer area near the brushed-stainless front door. Her dad was there, huddled with a couple of people in the nook he called the message center.

"Morning, Little Z," he said with that easy smile, the one that had been making fans swoon for the legendary Zac Trask since his first album way back in the dark ages. "You're up early. Sleep okay?"

Zara just shrugged, not interested in making small talk with her own father. "Where's Mickey?"

"Out running an errand," Zac said. "Lots to do before we leave."

Zara glanced at the huge whiteboard calendar that took up most of the wall. That was where everyone wrote down the details of Zac's schedule—concerts, meetings, publicity events, TV appearances, whatever.

Right now, most of the calendar was covered with two words written in Zac's messy scrawl: EUROPE, BABY!

Zara stared at the big matching star someone else had scribbled in the box for this coming Wednesday. In just three days, her dad and his posse would be in Amsterdam, partying like—well, like rock stars. Duh.

So why wasn't she tagging along? Zara had told everyone it was because she didn't want to miss the whole summer show season at her new barn. Maybe that was even true. Either way, she wasn't totally sure she was making the right choice.

Still, she figured it was a win-win. Her actress mother was in Vancouver shooting a movie for at least another month or two, which meant that once Zac left, Zara would be on her own. Well, except for whichever peons from his entourage he left behind to keep an eye on her. But they should be easy enough to whip into shape, and then? Party time in the loft every night.

"Whatever," she said. "Someone needs to drive me to the barn, or else I'm calling the car service." Stupid New York

City. She wasn't even allowed to think about driving in Manhattan until she turned seventeen, even though she'd had her permit already in California.

"Okay." It was pretty obvious by the faraway look in Zac's moss-green eyes that he hadn't heard a word. "Listen, Little Z. Been meaning to tell you something."

"What?" Zara started looking for her boots, which she was pretty sure she'd dropped in the foyer on her way in yesterday.

"Found someone to come stay with you while I'm gone."

His words were so casual, so offhand, that it took a second for them to sink in. Even then, Zara wasn't sure she'd heard him right.

"You what?" she said.

He shrugged. "You're only sixteen, right? What kind of parent would I be, leaving you all alone in the big bad city?"

One of Zac's assistants looked up from scrolling through the messages on the answering machine and chortled. "Good one, Zac."

Zara ignored the assistant, staring at her father. "What the hell are you talking about? I can stay by myself. It's not like I'm a child."

"Still, with me and your mom both so far away—"

"Please tell me you're shitting me," Zara said, the other people in the loft going silent as her voice got louder. "You didn't seriously hire, like, a babysitter to come change my diapers while Daddums is away? Give me a freaking break!"

"Chill out," Zac said. "It's not like that, okay? I'm not talking about paying some nanny or something."

"Then what *are* you talking about?" Zara crossed her arms over her chest and glared at him.

"She's a cousin of mine. Second cousin, actually. At least I think that's right." Zac scratched his chin, which sported a couple of days' worth of stubble. Carefully trimmed for maximum hunky effect, of course. "She's a college student. Very smart girl. She'll be graduating next year and wants to explore some career options here in NYC, so she's willing to come stay as long as we need her. Win-win, right?"

"Oh, sure." Zara's voice dripped with sarcasm. "I can't wait to get bossed around by some small-town brainiac nerd all summer. Sounds like a blast."

"Might as well drop the attitude, Little Z," Zac said, his voice taking on the steely, distant edge it always got when he was tired of sparring with her. "It's already settled. She gets here on Wednesday right before we leave."

TWO

——— ——— ——— ——— ———

Kate automatically flicked the lead out of Ford's way as the gelding stepped over to a tastier section of grass. But most of her attention was elsewhere. She was grazing Ford on the patch of lawn between the main barn and the large outdoor jumping arena, giving her the perfect view of Tommi's ride on Legs. Jamie was perched on the ring fence, watching every move horse and rider made.

"Nice," he called as Tommi and Legs finished a line of two jumps. "Take him around and try again. This time, do it in five strides instead of four."

Kate didn't get to see how Tommi and Legs did with the exercise. Just as they picked up a canter again, she heard a flurry of high-pitched barking from the direction of the barn. A fuzzy brown-and-white shape came streaking out, aiming straight at Ford.

"Whiskey, no!" Kate exclaimed, quickly taking up the slack in the lead line in case the gelding spooked. "Stay back."

The dog, a hard-eyed Jack Russell terrier wearing a pink collar studded with lime-green crystals, actually stopped and stared at her. That gave its owner, a blandly pretty blond girl a year younger than Kate, time to hurry out of the barn and scoop him into her arms.

"Naughty boy," Summer Campbell cooed into her dog's ear, hugging him so tightly that he squirmed with annoyance. "I told you not to run off!"

Kate wanted to shake her, even though Ford hadn't reacted except to lift his head and take a step back. It could have been a lot worse. That was why visiting dogs were supposed to stay on a leash—barn rules. But Summer never thought the rules applied to her.

"So what's going on out there?" Summer turned to stare at the ring. "Is Tommi having a private lesson?"

"Sort of, I guess," Kate said, keeping an eye on Whiskey as Ford went back to grazing. "Jamie's advising her on her training plan for Legs."

"Oh." Summer set her dog down as he started wriggling harder. He spotted a barn cat wandering past and took off after it, barking at the top of his lungs.

Kate winced, even though she knew the barn cat would be okay—thanks to his stubby legs and overfed belly, the obnoxious little dog hadn't managed to catch one yet. "Um, you might want to keep an eye on Whiskey," she said. "Joy's teaching the beginner adults in the flatwork ring right now, and if he spooks one of their horses . . ."

She let her voice trail off, since she could tell Summer wasn't listening. That happened a lot. Summer's parents had clawed their way into the privileged class in Manhattan on the healthy profits of their busy textile company. As a result, Summer seemed to think that anybody who couldn't afford custom Vogel field boots and a Devoucoux saddle wasn't worth her attention. Which made Kate pretty much invisible.

"I still don't know why Tommi wanted to buy a green horse like that when she already has her own nice made horses to show," Summer commented, watching as Legs circled around for another go at the jumps. "He's not even that nice looking. He's way skinnier and smaller than Toccata or her eq horse, or even her other jumper. If I didn't know better, I'd think he was a rescue horse or something instead of a show horse."

Kate didn't bother to answer. Of course Summer wouldn't see the point of Tommi getting a horse who didn't match the rest of her string. Or consider what a horse could do in the ring instead of what brand was on its butt. For some reason, she seemed to expect Tommi to be the same way.

But Tommi wasn't like that. That was why she and Kate were such good friends despite their very different backgrounds. Sure, Kate always felt a little weird when Tommi made some offhand comment about partying with the governor's daughter, or when she turned up at the barn wearing new custom half-chaps that had probably cost more than Kate made in a week. At least they were always comfortable when the subject was horses.

Thinking about that made Kate realize that things were pretty much the opposite with her other best friend, Natalie. Kate had been thinking about Nat a lot these past few days. The two of them had grown up together in their little blue-collar hometown just a few miles from Pelham Lane. They'd started riding together, too. Natalie still rode at their old lesson barn—and still didn't seem to get why Kate had wanted to move on. These days, when horses came up, things could get a little touchy. In fact, the two of them hadn't spoken in over a week—since the day Nat had called to invite Kate to a party, then gotten mad when Kate had told her she couldn't make it because of the Hounds Hollow show.

Kate bit her lip as she thought about the way Nat had hung up on her. She put her free hand in her pocket and touched her cell phone, wondering if she should call Nat now, see if she was ready to make up.

"Looks like they're finished," Summer said, breaking into her thoughts.

Kate glanced at the ring. Tommi had dismounted and was running up her stirrups. Feeling sort of relieved, Kate pulled her hand out of her pocket. Calling Nat would have to wait.

"Looking good, Tommi!" Summer called out as horse and rider walked toward them on their way to the barn door. "Your new horse is gorgeous. And are those new breeches? They look like the new Tailored Sportsmans; are they? They're fabulous on you."

"Thanks," Tommi said without bothering to answer the girl's questions. She smiled at Kate. "What'd you think? He's really starting to trust me on our distances."

"I could tell," Kate said. "All the flatwork you've been doing is paying off."

Jamie had paused behind the others to check his messages, but now he hurried over. "Kate," he said. "I'm glad you're here. I'd like to talk to you about something, if you've got a moment."

"Um, sure," Kate said, switching Ford's lead to her other hand and shooting Tommi a nervous look. Tommi shrugged slightly, then moved on with both Legs and Summer trailing behind her.

When Kate turned back to Jamie, she was relieved to see that he was smiling. Good. At least that meant he probably wasn't about to ream her out for screwing something up. He trusted her with a lot of responsibility around the barn—almost as much as his senior grooms, Miguel and Elliot, who'd both been with him for over ten years. Kate always tried to live up to that trust, but sometimes it made her feel like a juggler with too many plates in the air, certain that at least one of them was about to come crashing down any minute now.

"Thanks for taking such good care of Ford," Jamie said, stepping over to give the gelding a rub on the neck. Ford ignored him, tugging at his lead as he stretched toward a tasty patch of clover. "I know the Halls really appreciate all the extra attention you've been giving him since he got hurt."

Kate just nodded, trying not to let her emotions show on her face. Ford belonged to Fitz's parents now. They'd bought him from his previous owners right after Hounds Hollow, paying the gelding's former asking price even though he'd probably never be worth anything close to that again. Kate still had trouble believing that one evening in the hay stall at Hounds Hollow had led to this. It remained a little painful for her to think about what had happened that night, the night of the party and Ford's accident, the night that had left Kate feeling

22

used—and worse yet, stupid. Stupid for trusting Fitz, for believing that a hound dog could change his ways.

But the very next day, Fitz had surprised her again. They were all upset about what had happened to Ford—and even more so about Zara's threat to tell Jamie that everyone's favorite new groom was in the country illegally if they spilled the beans. Just when Tommi and Kate had almost convinced Zara to confess, Fitz had come along with Jamie—and before the rest of them knew what was happening, he'd confessed to the Ford incident himself!

Kate knew the others still didn't quite understand why he'd done it. But she knew. He'd done it for her. It was his twisted, Fitz-like way of proving that he'd do anything to win her trust back.

"But that's not what I wanted to talk to you about," Jamie went on, glancing quickly at his cell phone as it buzzed, then tucking it away again without answering. "We haven't had much chance to chat since Hounds Hollow, but I've been thinking about you and Fable."

Fabelhaften, better known as Fable, was a sales horse that Jamie had just started letting Kate ride in the hypercompetitive 3'6" junior equitation division known as the Big Eq. The big gray gelding's owner had moved overseas and was footing all the bills until Fable sold, which meant Kate didn't even have to worry about paying entry fees. It was an amazing opportunity, and she knew she'd never be able to work hard enough to pay Jamie back for it.

"I'm really pleased with how you did with him," Jamie went on. "Not many new horse-and-rider teams actually pin in their first attempt at the Big Eq, especially when neither of them has ever done it before."

"Thanks," Kate said softly. "Fable's a really talented horse."

"I know he is. And I can already tell I was right about you being a good match for him." He smiled. "That means it's time to talk about next steps for you two."

"Good boy," Tommi crooned as she ran a brush over Legs's already gleaming back. "You were a superstar today, you know that?"

The lean bay gelding shifted impatiently in the cross-ties. He hated standing still for long, even when he was tired, and could be a handful when he got bored with being groomed. Or led. Or ridden, for that matter.

But Tommi didn't mind any of that. Quirky was okay, as long as the horse could back it up in the ring. And this one could. After today's ride, she was more certain of it than ever.

Just then Kate hurried around the corner. "Hi," she said. "Need some help?"

"Sure, if you've got time." Tommi tossed her another brush from the grooming tote at her feet. "Thought you were still out grazing Ford."

"I just put him back in his stall." Kate went to work on Legs's other side.

Tommi could tell her friend had something on her mind. But when it came to sharing her thoughts, Kate could be as spooky as a fresh horse on a windy day, so Tommi kept quiet as long as she could stand it.

After a minute or two of silence, her patience ran out. "So what'd Jamie want to talk to you about?" she asked.

"Oh." Kate glanced up. "Um, just about where he wants me to go with Fable. He's entering us in the eq again at the show this week."

"Totally not surprised. Wish I'd seen your round last time— I heard you two did great."

Tommi smiled, suddenly flashing back to the memory of Kate when she'd first arrived at Pelham Lane a couple of years earlier, fresh from that backyard lesson mill of hers. Some of the other riders had snickered about her faded no-name jods and battered paddock boots, the way she barely spoke above a whisper and called Jamie "sir," and how she always ended up with hay, shavings, and/or horse slobber in her blond hair by the end of the day.

But Jamie had believed in her and given her the chance to prove him right. And Kate had. Big-time. These days, she still only had one good pair of breeches and regularly walked around with hay stuck in her ponytail. But nobody could imagine Pelham Lane without her.

"So is he thinking you two might be able to qualify for any of the finals this year?" Tommi asked Kate.

Kate shrugged, then glanced up as a burst of laughter came from the end of the aisle. A second later Marissa rounded the corner, along with another junior rider named Dani.

"Hi, guys," Marissa said when she saw Tommi and Kate. "What's up?"

"Kate was just telling me about Jamie's big plans for her in the Big Eq," Tommi replied, reaching up to flick some dust off

Legs's haunches. "He's already mapping out their triumphant journey to finals."

"Yeah, congrats again on that ribbon last weekend, Kate," Dani said.

"And thanks for making the rest of us look bad," Marissa added with a playful groan. "Now I've got no excuse for never pinning in the eq. Well, except not being as tall and skinny as you—I keep telling Jamie I've got a medical condition that requires me to eat at least fifteen bagels a week, but I'm not sure he believes me."

Dani laughed, and Tommi rolled her eyes. Marissa was always joking around about her weight and her many failed attempts to diet, even though she wasn't even really heavy— just not built naturally long and lean like Kate.

Kate smiled, looking a little uncomfortable, then bent to grab a different brush out of Tommi's tote. Meanwhile Dani stepped over to give Legs a pat.

"How's your new guy doing, Tommi?" she asked.

"Great," Tommi said. "Most of the time, anyway. He's still having quite a few greenie moments, though. I was actually sort of wondering if I should skip this next show, give him a break. Maybe just work at home this week, then have both of us take the weekend off."

"Really?" Marissa sounded surprised. "You mean you wouldn't go to the show at all? Even to ride your other horses?"

"Is that what Jamie suggested today?" Kate asked. "Giving Legs a week off? You didn't mention that."

"No, Jamie didn't suggest it. It's just something I've been thinking about." Tommi was already wishing she hadn't said anything.

But now that it was out there, she had to wonder. The idea had seemed perfectly logical in her head. But was it really what she thought was best for Legs? Or was she mostly thinking about herself—specifically, that Hamptons trip and the chance to spend the whole week getting to know Alex better instead of just a couple of days? It would be so easy to make it happen. Jamie's assistant trainer, Joy, always stayed home from shows to keep the barn running. Tommi could ask her to school Legs a few times, or maybe just lunge him to keep him in shape . . .

The buzz of her cell phone broke into her thoughts. Grabbing the phone out of her pocket, she saw that it was a text from Grant.

Hi! What's up? Party was fun last night, huh?

Tommi frowned. Uh-oh. She and Grant were still friends. But not the type of friends that sent chatty texts to each other for no reason. Had seeing her at that party rekindled his interest in her? She hoped not—telling him she didn't like him in that way had been uncomfortable enough the first time. She didn't want to do it again.

"Everything okay, Tommi?" Marissa asked.

Tommi glanced up quickly, remembering she wasn't alone. Marissa was watching her face curiously. The girl liked to play the clown most of the time, but Tommi knew she wasn't nearly as ditzy as she let on. And she loved any hint of gossip.

"Oh. No, I'm fine," Tommi said, quickly pasting on the neutral expression she'd perfected after so many years of living in her family. She reached out to unclip the closest cross-tie. "Just thinking it's probably time to get Legs put away."

Halfway to the gelding's stall, she heard her phone buzz

again. She waited until she got Legs settled, then checked the message as she stepped toward the aisle. It was another text from Grant: *By the way, do u have Zara's #? I might give her a call if u don't mind.*

Tommi paused in the stall doorway, staring at the message. Zara? He wanted Zara's number?

She flashed back to the party at the hotel the last night of Hounds Hollow. Zara and Grant had ended up in a serious make-out session in the pool. Tommi had assumed it was just a little drunken fun, but could it have been more than that, at least for Grant? Could he really be interested in Zara?

And why shouldn't he be? Zara had inherited the best of both her parents' looks—flawless dark skin and glossy black curls from her gorgeous Trinidadian actress mother, striking green eyes and a strong chin from her ruggedly handsome father. Tommi wasn't sure which side of the family the big boobs came from, but whatever. She was pretty sure the guys didn't care where they came from.

But Grant wasn't totally shallow, at least Tommi didn't think so. One drunken evening wasn't enough for him to know what Zara was really like. Tommi still wasn't sure she knew herself. Everyone had known Zara's rep since long before she'd moved to Jamie's barn—the bad girl, the celebubrat from LA who did whatever she wanted and screw the consequences. Tommi knew better than to assume that anyone's public image was totally true, even if most of the others didn't. She knew people were more complicated than that.

But was Zara the exception to that rule? At first it had sort of seemed like it. Tommi had been ready to write her off, especially after the disaster with Ford. But then Zara had stepped up, ready to confess to Jamie what she'd done. Fitz had jumped in before she got the chance—Tommi still wasn't sure what to think about *that*, but Fitz was another topic—and so Jamie still didn't know the truth. But the important thing was that she'd been willing to do it. That had won her more than a few points in Tommi's eyes.

Was it enough to make up for all the other crap? Tommi wasn't sure yet. She bit her lip, feeling oddly uncomfortable. Why did Grant have to put her in the middle of this? He was one of her oldest friends, and she didn't want to see him get hurt.

But she quickly shook that off. Grant was a big boy—he could take care of himself. Giving Legs a pat, she fastened his stall guard, then headed to the office to get Zara's number. As soon as she had it, she texted it to Grant, trying not to think about it too much.

Her phone was hardly back in her pocket for five seconds before it buzzed again. This time it was a phone call. Tommi didn't even bother to check the screen, figuring it was Grant calling to thank her. He was just that kind of guy.

"Hi," she said.

"Tommi? Is that you? Hi!"

Tommi blinked. That definitely wasn't Grant, but it took her a second to place the voice.

"Alex?" she said, her stomach doing a funny little flip. "Hey! What's up?"

"Hope you don't mind me calling," he said. "Parker gave me your number. I just came up with an idea and wanted to run it by you."

"Sure," Tommi said. "What is it?"

"Think I already told you, I'm crashing at a friend's place in the city this weekend," he said. "I was going to hop the Jitney back home on Monday, but then Parker said you'd probably drive yourself out for the house party."

"That's the plan," Tommi said. "Want a ride?"

"That's what I was hoping you'd say." She could almost hear his grin through the phone. "I'm seriously bummed that you have to cut out early for your show, but at least this way I'll get to hang with you a little longer, you know?"

"Sounds fun," Tommi said. "It's a date." Then, realizing a half second too late what she'd said, she gulped. "Um, I mean, you know—"

"No, it's okay," he said quickly. "It's definitely a date. If that's okay with you. You know."

"Yeah." Tommi felt awkward. She was usually better than this at talking to guys.

Then Alex laughed sheepishly. "Okay, how'd this conversation suddenly go all middle-school dance on us? Or is it just me?"

"Nope." Tommi laughed, too. "Not just you. So let's review here: I'm driving out to the Hamptons, you're coming along. Deal?"

"Deal," Alex said. "Hey, and if you've got an iPod dock in your car, how about I bring some stuff to listen to? I want you to hear that band I was telling you about at the party. I think you'll really like them."

"Cool," Tommi said. "But I should probably warn you—if I don't like something, I don't fake it. If your favorite band sucks, I'm going to say so."

"You'd better," Alex retorted quickly. "I'm not much into pushovers or fakers. I could tell you weren't like that as soon as I met you. It's what made me want to find out more."

"Okay, good." Tommi felt a little shiver of anticipation run through her. She was looking forward to finding out more, too. "So what's this band like again?"

She was smiling when she hung up a few minutes later. So maybe her idea to skip the show entirely was kind of lame. But compromising by going out a couple of days later than she'd originally planned?

Yeah, that seemed to be working out just right.

THREE

——— ——— ——— ——— ———

"Zara! Hi!" Summer was in the aisle watching Max sweep when Zara entered the barn. "I was hoping you'd come out today. Did you get my text?" She hurried toward Zara, her obnoxious little brat of a dog leaping at her heels.

Great. Just what Zara needed to make her foul mood even worse. Summer was like the ugly chin zit you assumed would go away if you ignored it long enough. Only it didn't. Just kept getting bigger and more disgusting.

"Nope, didn't get any text from you," Zara lied. "Your phone must be screwed up or something."

Summer's pale blue eyes widened with alarm. "Do you really think so?" she exclaimed, fishing a shiny new pink cell phone out of the pocket of her Tailored Sportsmans. "But I just got it! It's exactly like the one Tommi has—well, except hers is boring black—so I figured it was probably, like, really good . . ."

Zara hardly heard her. Her mind was already wandering

back to her father's big news. Yeah, leave it to Zac to think she'd actually be okay with having a babysitter while he was in Europe. Clueless didn't even begin to cover it.

But whatever. It looked like she'd just be spending even more time at the barn than usual. At least for the rest of the summer.

As she wandered off down the aisle, she realized Summer was tagging along at her heels as obsessively as her bratty little dog might do. And yapping nonstop just like him, too. Did she even notice that Zara wasn't listening?

". . . and anyway, I heard Fitz is, like, totally grounded from the next show," Summer was saying as Zara tuned back in. "I wonder if—"

"That's nice." Zara cut her off. "Got to run. Ellie's probably waiting for me. And she hates to wait."

Both those things were true, at least. Zara had called ahead from the car to ask the grooms to get the mare ready. And Ellie tended to get testy if left in the cross-ties for half a second longer than she felt was necessary.

Zara couldn't help smiling as she thought about her new horse. Yeah, so maybe that last show hadn't gone as smoothly as it could have. But that was part of the fun, right? At least Ellie had a mind of her own. Zara was already looking forward to the next show when the two of them could show everyone what they could *really* do.

"Oh, you mean you're going for a ride right now?" Summer asked eagerly.

"Um, duh," Zara said. "Why do you think I came to the barn? To get a mani-pedi?"

Summer appeared totally unfazed by the sarcasm. "Cool, I was thinking about riding soon, too. I'll join you."

Zara bit her tongue—literally—to stop herself from snapping out a rude reply. Sure, Summer was a pain in the ass. But she wasn't really the one who was making Zara feel like crap. Nope, that honor belonged to her own father, the guy who barely noticed where she went or what she did—and yet suddenly seemed to think she needed to be treated like a five-year-old.

"Whatever," she muttered as Summer hurried off down the barn aisle shouting for Miguel.

Zara turned toward Ellie's stall. The mare was cross-tied in the aisle, with Zara's saddle already neatly positioned atop a spotless Mattes pad. Javier was bent over the horse's front legs fiddling with her sheepskin-lined Eskadron boots.

When she saw the young groom, Zara's stomach twisted as she instantly flashed back to the Hounds Hollow showgrounds. The drunken crash. The injured horse. Her desperate threat to turn Javier in, tell Jamie he was illegal. How long had it taken for someone to tell Javier about that? Whatever, he had to know all about it by now. All about how she'd almost ruined his life.

One of the barn dogs, Hugo, was sitting nearby chewing on a stray bit of hoof the farrier must've tossed him. The dog wagged his tail and jumped to his feet when he noticed Zara coming, which made Javier look up as well.

"Hi, Miss Trask," the groom said politely, his dark eyes unreadable behind their long lashes. "She's almost ready for you."

"Thanks," Zara muttered, not quite meeting his gaze.

He finished adjusting the boot and stood. "Are you ready?" he asked. "I'll bridle her for you now if you like."

"Sure, thanks."

Javier hurried off toward the tack room with Hugo right behind him, leaving Zara standing there feeling guilty and unsettled as she wondered what the young groom was thinking about her right now. Ugh. And this was supposed to be her refuge from the annoyances of home?

Just then Fitz wandered into view at the end of the aisle. Great. Another person she definitely didn't feel like dealing with right now. She'd barely seen him since the end of the show, mostly because his parents had banned him from the barn for a week once they heard what had happened. Well, what had *supposedly* happened.

Zara still couldn't believe he'd jumped in to cover for her. The weirdest part was that he hadn't even done it to try to get in her pants. That would have been better, actually. She would've known how to handle that.

This? Not so much. She didn't like owing anyone anything.

"Hey, good lookin'. What's cookin'?" Fitz quipped when he got closer. "Didn't know you were here today."

"Sorry, guess I forgot to alert the media," she muttered.

It came out sounding more sour than funny, but Fitz laughed anyway. "How's Ellie today?" he asked, stepping over to give the mare a scratch on the withers. She turned her head as far as the cross-ties would allow, nuzzling him in obvious hope of scoring a treat.

Zara didn't answer. Javier had just returned with her bridle. He expertly slipped it on, then handed over the reins.

"Do you need anything else, Miss Trask?" he asked in his soft voice.

"No, I'm good." Zara forced a smile. "Thanks."

"See you, Javier," Fitz said. As soon as the groom disappeared around the corner, he glanced at Zara. "Hey, guess what?"

"Do I have to?" Zara jammed her helmet on and clicked the throat snap shut.

"What? No, seriously." Fitz lowered his voice. "I was talking to Max, and he said nobody ever told Javier what happened that night. You know—what you said about him."

Zara spun around to face him. "Wait, for real?" she said. "Come on. This place is gossip central. How could he not know?"

Fitz lifted one shoulder, then let it drop. "Guess the other guys didn't want to freak him out. I told Max you were never going to actually rat Javier out to Jamie, anyway. So no harm, no foul. At least for that part."

Zara wasn't sure how to respond, so she didn't. Just turned and lifted the saddle flap, pretending to check her girth.

After a moment of silence, Fitz cleared his throat. "Anyway, I just thought you'd like to know," he said. "Gotta go. Have a good ride, okay?"

"Thanks," Zara muttered without taking her eyes off the girth.

She wasn't going to let Fitz know it, but her mood had just ticked up a notch. Okay, so all the other juniors still knew exactly what she'd done, plus now she had this new garbage at home to deal with. But at least she wouldn't have to feel guilty every time she looked at Javier from now on.

At least there was that.

Soon she was leading Ellie outside. The assistant trainer was teaching a bunch of bratty tweens in the big jumping ring, so Zara kept going to the next ring. A couple of adult amateurs were in there schooling their horses. So was Summer, mounted on a chunky bay that Zara was pretty sure was her large junior hunter. Not that she paid much attention to anything having to do with Summer.

"In here, Zara!" Summer called, waving her hand.

Zara almost turned and kept going. But why bother? She'd grown up learning to ignore pushy paparazzi and obnoxious fans. Summer was nothing.

"Come on, girlie," she whispered to Ellie, leading her in and turning toward the mounting block.

"Hurry up, Zara! Maybe we can do like a fake pairs class or something. Wouldn't that be fun?"

"Watch where you're going," one of the adults snapped loudly, swinging her horse out to avoid running into Summer, who'd just turned sharply toward the center of the ring without looking.

Zara hid a smirk by fiddling with her stirrup. She'd vaguely noticed that particular adult ammy at the shows, a woman in her thirties with a cocky attitude and a foul mouth. She was some kind of big-shot lawyer or something—what was her name again? Mary, Marcy?

"Sorry, Margie," Summer said.

Margie had cantered down toward the other end of the ring by now, catching up to the other ammy, an older woman on a placid-looking gray. Summer halted and watched Zara mount.

"Hold still, girl," Zara ordered as Ellie danced in place

beside the mounting block. She managed to get her left foot in the stirrup and swing aboard, but her horse immediately trotted off with her head in the air.

"You shouldn't let her do that," Summer said. "Jamie says they're supposed to stand until you tell them to move off."

Zara had already started shortening her reins, preparing to halt. But she wasn't about to let Summer think she was taking riding advice from the likes of her. So instead, she gave Ellie a sharp kick.

The mare flung her head in the air and broke into a choppy canter. Zara had to squeeze with both legs to stay on, since she hadn't really gotten her seat yet—or even picked up her right stirrup. Her tight leg—or maybe that flapping stirrup—made Ellie even more agitated, and soon she was bolting straight across the ring.

"Settle down, dammit!" Zara exclaimed, fishing for the stirrup as best she could. She finally caught it and stood in both stirrups, hauling on the reins.

"Look out!" a frightened voice called.

Zara looked up. Ellie was headed straight toward the older adult ammy. All Zara knew about her was that her name was Mrs. Walsh and she was some kind of rich New York socialite. Oh, and that she was one of those chickenshit adult riders who preferred her horses one step livelier than dead. Yeah, running over someone like her wasn't exactly the best way for Zara to stay on Jamie's good side.

"Whoa, you stupid thing!" Zara cried, struggling to pull Ellie into a circle.

The mare fought her hands and legs, skittering sideways

with her head cranked to the side. She almost crashed into the other horse before giving in and circling away. Mrs. Walsh's gray gelding actually woke up long enough to lift his head, swish his tail, and take a lazy step sideways.

"Whoa, whoa!" Mrs. Walsh exclaimed, sounding terrified. "Easy, boy."

Meanwhile Summer and Margie were both watching from nearby. Summer just sat there staring. But Margie kicked her horse forward.

"Get a grip!" she yelled at Zara. "If you can't control your horse, you shouldn't be riding in a ring with other people!" She turned toward Mrs. Walsh. "You okay, Elaine?" she asked in a quieter tone.

Zara didn't stick around to hear any more. Ellie had finally slowed to a walk, and Zara aimed her toward the gate.

"Where are you going?" Summer called, pushing her own horse to follow.

Zara leaned down to swing open the gate from the saddle, just the way she'd learned from an old cowboy on one of her mother's movie sets. "Out," she said. "I'm not in the mood for this. I'm going on a trail ride."

Summer's eyes widened. "Are you sure that's a good idea?" she said. "Ellie seems kind of worked up, and she probably hasn't ridden out much. If it were me, I'd be kind of nervous, you know?"

"Good thing it's not you, then," Zara snapped. She nudged Ellie through the gate, then swung it closed behind her, not wanting Summer to get any bright ideas about tagging along.

In her current mood, she might have almost enjoyed

continuing the battle with her horse in the great wide open. But to her surprise, Ellie seemed to relax as soon as they were away from the ring. She stopped fighting Zara's aids and settled into a loose, swinging walk, pricking her ears at everything they passed—a couple of barn dogs wrestling in the grass, a bird perched on a fence, a stall cleaner dumping his wheelbarrow in the manure pit.

"Well, what do you know," Zara murmured, turning the mare down the grassy lane between two turnout fields. "So Miss Fancypants really wants to be a trail horse. Who knew?"

Just then Ellie snorted and spooked at a squirrel, and Zara laughed. Okay, so the mare still had some spunk. But that was okay. It was one of the things Zara liked about her.

She ended up spending more than an hour exploring the sprawling property with Ellie. They trotted through an empty pasture and jumped the coop set in the fence line for the local foxhunters; they galloped up the steep hill near the creek, then wandered along a couple of wooded trails to cool down. By the time Zara reluctantly headed back in, her mood had turned around completely.

"I'm glad I came to ride today, girlie," she told Ellie, reaching forward to give her a pat. "Sorry about earlier. But this was fun."

Yeah, there was still the thing with her dad to worry about. Not to mention the knowledge that if anyone told Jamie what had really happened that night at the showgrounds, she was toast. But it wasn't like she could do much about either of those things. So why stress?

As she led Ellie into the barn a few minutes later, she saw

Tommi coming out of the tack room. "Hi," Tommi said. "Summer said you were here somewhere."

Her tone was friendly, so Zara cautiously returned her smile. Tommi was hard to figure sometimes. Okay, make that most of the time. It seemed like the two of them had butted heads pretty much since Zara had arrived at Pelham Lane, though things had been better since the Hounds Hollow show.

"Yeah, figured I'd get some saddle time in before the horses leave for the show tomorrow," Zara said. "You?"

"Same, pretty much." Tommi shrugged. "When are you heading down?"

"Thursday, I guess." Zara frowned, realizing that her father was leaving for Amsterdam on Wednesday. Along with his driver, Mickey, who usually drove her to the barn and to shows. Was this country cousin of hers supposed to be her chauffeur as well as her babysitter? Or what? "If I find a ride, that is," she muttered, a little of her bad mood creeping back.

"You don't have a ride?" Tommi said. "You can bum one with me if you want. I'm spending a couple of days in the Hamptons, so I won't be leaving the city until Thursday morning myself."

"Really? Cool," Zara said. "Guess that could work out."

"Okay, I'll call you Wednesday and let you know what time to be ready." Tommi started to turn away, then paused. "By the way, hope you don't mind. Grant asked for your number, so I gave it to him."

"Grant?" For a second Zara drew a blank. Then she remembered—that was Tommi's preppy friend's name. She had a vague memory of him feeling her up in the hotel pool. He wasn't a bad kisser. "Oh, right. Yeah, it's cool—thanks."

She was smiling again as she and Tommi parted ways. Yeah, this day wasn't turning out all bad after all.

She was smiling again as she and Tommi parted ways.

"So how's that horse of ours doing?"

Tommi glanced up as she slid into her seat at the dining room table. She'd arrived home from the barn half an hour earlier, which had just given her time to shower and start packing for the Hamptons trip before the housekeeper had called her to dinner.

"He's fine," she told her father. "I'll be taking him in the jumpers again this weekend."

"Oh, so you're going to a horse show this week?" her stepmother said, reaching for the dish of roasted asparagus that Mrs. Grigoryan had just set on the table. "I thought you were taking a week off to go to the Hamptons."

"Not the whole week. I'm meeting the barn at the show on Thursday, remember?"

"Good," her father said. "Any nibbles yet?"

Tommi wanted to roll her eyes, but stopped herself. "Not yet," she said. "But he's only been to one show so far since we've owned him."

"Hmmph." Her father seemed to lose interest as he speared a crab cake with his fork and slapped it on his plate. He turned and started talking to his wife about some art gallery opening they were going to soon, and Tommi slumped in her chair, off the hot seat—at least for now.

She toyed with her food, feeling uneasy as she realized her father wasn't going to let up on her until Legs was sold. He wasn't exactly known for his patience, either on Wall Street or around home. Whatever. It was the price she had to pay. But it made her wonder yet again if it had been a mistake to cut her show week short because of that Hamptons trip. Tommi wasn't used to second-guessing herself—usually once she made a decision, she just went with it. Full steam ahead, no regrets.

But this felt different somehow. Way more serious and grown-up. And suddenly it just seemed way too stressful to worry about, especially when she had more interesting things on her mind.

Like what she was going to wear for that long, cozy car ride with Alex tomorrow, for instance.

She smiled, mentally skimming through her closet. Her new flirty print sundress, maybe? Or the cute denim capris and a sexy tank? Now that was the kind of decision she had no trouble making.

Kate was surprised to see her father's car parked in front of the house when she got home that night. Usually he worked the night shift on Sundays.

Then she remembered him grumbling at dinner last week—something about how the new lieutenant was messing with people's schedules and otherwise shaking things up. Thinking about that made Kate's stomach twist with anxiety. Ever since her mom had gotten laid off from her part-time receptionist job when Kate was nine, any change of that sort made her anxious. But she tried not to dwell. It wasn't like she could do anything about it.

Besides, she was way too tired to worry about it right now. It had been a busy day at the barn as always, plus she'd stayed extra late helping pack up. They were leaving for the show the next day, and there never seemed to be enough time to get everything done.

The only light in the house was coming from the kitchen at the back. Kate headed that way, a little nervous about what she might find.

When she entered, her mother was standing at the sink scrubbing at a crusty saucepan. Kate felt her shoulders relax. Okay, so maybe most people didn't do the dishes at 1:00 a.m. But for Kate's mother, that almost passed as normal.

"Hi, Mom," Kate said, dropping her bag and sinking down onto one of the stools in front the battered butcher-block kitchen island.

"Katie! You're home." Her mother turned and smiled, her thin face tired but alert. "I was just starting to worry."

"You know you can call me whenever," Kate reminded her. "I always keep my phone on."

"I know. But I don't like to bother you." Her mother set down the pan and peeled off her rubber gloves. "Are you hungry? I can make you a plate. There's leftovers from dinner—we had that roast chicken your father likes so much."

"Thanks. That sounds great." As her mother hurried over to the refrigerator, Kate's mind drifted back to Pelham Lane and everything she had to do the next day. She loved shows, but sometimes she hated them, too. She especially hated hearing some of the other juniors complain about how it was *so* stressful having to show their hunters and then rush to warm up their eq horses, with barely enough time to have lunch and gossip with their friends in between. What did they know about stress?

She snapped out of it when her mother set a plate in front of her. "There you go, Katie," she said, already bustling back over to the fridge. "Just let me grab you some juice."

Kate's heart sank as she looked at the plate. Anyone else might not have noticed anything off about it. It was just a plate of chicken, carrots, and new potatoes.

No, the food itself wasn't the strange part. It was the way her mother had arranged it on the plate. Carefully, with none of the different foods touching each other. Exactly four pieces of chicken cut into the same size strips. Four chunks of carrot. Four potatoes.

In other words, business as usual. Kate had never even heard of OCD when her mother had started her rituals a few years earlier. All she'd known was that Mom had some funny habits, and it made Dad tense. Now, they were all so used to it that Kate sometimes wondered how much her father and younger brother even noticed anymore.

But *she* noticed. And it was getting harder and harder to take.

"There you are, sweetie." Her mother set a glass of juice beside the plate. Then she grabbed a rag and wiped off the countertop nearby. One circle, two, three, four.

Kate's fist clenched around her fork; she was too tired and stressed to deal with this right now. She wanted to rebel against her mother's cheery facade, let her know she knew what was going on, even if the only way she could think of to do it was to shove the piles of food into each other to see how her mother would react. She actually lifted the fork to do it.

But her hand froze in midair, the fork poised half an inch above the carrots. She couldn't follow through on the plan. It felt physically impossible.

"Just leave your dishes in the sink please, Katie," her mother said, completely unaware of Kate's struggle. "See you in the morning."

"Uh-huh." Kate didn't take her eyes off the food. Her hand had started shaking.

What was wrong with her? Was she turning into her crazy mother? Was it genetic?

Kate heard her mother open the door to the bedroom across the narrow back hall, releasing the sounds of her father's rhythmic snoring. As soon as the door closed again, Kate threw the fork aside and pushed back from the island, her heart pounding.

Dumping the food in the trash bin, she grabbed a soda and headed upstairs to her room in the bungalow's gabled half-story. So much for thinking, however briefly, that her mother might actually be getting better. She should know better than to get her hopes up.

Her father was asleep, and her brother wasn't much use lately. So Kate pulled out her phone and called the only other person who knew about her mom; the only other person who was probably still up at this hour.

"Kate?" Natalie's familiar voice said into her ear a second later. Sure enough, she sounded wide awake. "What's up?"

"I'm sorry," Kate blurted out. "I've been meaning to call you all week—I hate it when we fight, you know that."

"What?" Nat sounded confused for a second. "Oh, wait—is this about you flaking out on that party at the barn the other weekend? Don't worry, I'm over it." She laughed. "Actually that party was kind of a bust. The Tanners asked this crotchety old neighbor guy to stop by and check on things, and he chased us off before things could barely get started."

"Oh," Kate said softly. "That's too bad."

"Katie?" Nat's voice went sharp and curious. "You okay, babe? You sound weird."

"Yeah. I mean no. Not really." Kate took a long, shaky breath. "It's just, you know, Mom."

"Back on the crazy train, huh?" Though Natalie's words were snarky, her tone was sympathetic. "Sorry. That really sucks. You want to talk about it?"

"Not really," Kate said, sinking down on the edge of her bed and kicking off her paddock boots. "I mean, there's not much to say."

"Okay. But listen, talking horses always cheers you up, right? Just wait until you hear about the newest horse at Happy Acres. Thoroughbred. Only off the track a few weeks. And guess who's in charge of his training?"

"You?" Kate asked. She tried to sound cheerful, though secretly she was wincing. Nat was a decent rider, all things considered, athletic and pretty much fearless. But she had a temper and a touchy ego. A fresh ex-racehorse could be a disaster if things didn't go perfectly.

But Kate wasn't about to say so. Natalie didn't take criticism too well at the best of times. Especially riding criticism, and especially from Kate.

"Yeah, Mrs. Tanner told me I can make him my special project for the summer." Natalie sounded pleased with herself. "I'm even taking him in his first ever show in a couple of weeks."

"Show?" Kate echoed, leaning back against her pillow.

"Uh-huh. Just the summer schooling show at the barn, but still. Should be an adventure." Nat chuckled. "Hey, why don't you come watch? You haven't been back to one of our shows in ages."

"Oh." Kate bit her lip, hoping she wasn't about to piss Nat off again just when they'd finally made up. "Um, when is it?"

"Saturday after next."

Kate realized that was a nonshowing weekend for Pelham Lane. Still, she hesitated for a second, not sure what to say. Saturday was always a busy day at the barn, and Jamie counted on her being around to help out.

But maybe she could swing it somehow. It might be worth juggling her schedule just this once, if it meant getting her friendship with Natalie back on track.

"That might work," she said. "I'll try to be there."

FOUR

———   ———   ———   ———   ———

Perfect. If Tommi had to use only one word to describe the evening, that would be it. Perfect. She couldn't think of a single thing that could be better, a single place she'd rather be right now.

She took a sip of her beer and glanced around. It was Monday evening, and the house party had moved to the pristine private beach behind Alex's house. Alex and the other guys had lit a bonfire, which crackled away and cast a warm orange glow over the pale sand. The last rays of the setting sun had disappeared a while ago, though Tommi wasn't sure what time it was—she'd forgotten to put her watch back on after taking a dip in the pool earlier. She also hadn't bothered to change out of her swimsuit—none of them had—though she'd shrugged on a loose linen shirt as a cover-up against the cool evening breeze coming off the ocean.

Stretching her bare legs out in the teak chair she'd dragged down from the pool deck, Tommi dug her toes into the sand

and smiled as she watched Alex rummaging around in the cooler at the end of the weathered wooden walkway leading down over the dunes from his massive shingle-style house. The two of them had spent the long car ride across Long Island talking about everything and anything. School. Music. Friends. Family. Horses. Life in general.

"So." Courtney leaned over from her chair nearby. "You and Alex, huh?"

Tommi shrugged, not bothering to be coy. "We'll see. He's cool."

"Definitely." Court took a chug of her beer. "The first time I saw him, I told Parker he'd better watch out. With something that hot around, I might decide to trade up if he gets on my nerves too much."

Tommi laughed. Before she could answer, Alex was back, clutching two dripping beers in one hand.

"Looks like we're out of light," he said. "Regular okay?"

"Sure." Tommi took the beer, even though she hadn't finished her first yet.

Just then they all heard a loud whoop. There was a flurry of movement on the ocean side of the fire. Tommi squinted, but couldn't tell what was going on beyond the glare of the flames.

But Court stood up for a better look. "Oh, man," she said, tugging at the top of her bandeau swimsuit. "Looks like Duckface decided to go skinny-dipping."

Within moments almost everyone was gathered at the surf line, watching and cheering as Duckface frolicked in the waves. Tommi stood and stretched, not really in the mood. It wasn't as if she'd never seen Duckface naked before. The boy had been pulling the same stunt for as long as she'd known him.

Luckily Alex seemed to be on the same wavelength. "Want to go for a walk?" he asked quietly.

Soon the two of them were strolling down the beach with the waves lapping at their feet. The sounds of the party faded behind them as they passed one beachfront estate after another. Most of the houses had lights on, but there was nobody else out on the beach, making it feel almost as if Tommi and Alex were the only two people in the world.

"What a gorgeous night," Tommi said, breathing in the sweet-sour scents of sand and sea. "Almost makes me want to ditch the city and move out here."

"You totally should." Alex leaned close enough to bump her shoulder with his as they walked. "Anyway, I'm glad you decided to come out, even if it's just for a couple of days."

"Me too." Tommi meant it. Still, his words had reminded her of what she could—should?—be doing instead, and she couldn't help wondering how things were going at the show-grounds. What had Jamie really thought when she'd told him she wasn't turning up until Thursday this time? Would Legs get antsy cooped up in a show stall without her there to hand walk and ride him to keep his restless mind occupied?

"Hey." Alex reached over and caught her hand, turning her to face him. "You okay? You, like, went a million miles away all of a sudden."

"Sorry." Tommi smiled at him, feeling a little sheepish. "I really am glad I came. Thanks for inviting me, this is great. I'm just maybe feeling a little guilty about ditching the first part of my show."

He squeezed her hand, his palm warm in hers and scratchy with sand. "I know you're totally serious about riding and everything. But I guess I don't get it. There'll be another show soon, right? Is it really that big a deal to miss a couple of days of this one?"

"No. I mean, yes. Kind of." Tommi hesitated, not sure how honestly she wanted to answer. She'd already told him about Legs, including the part about her father putting up some of the money. But she hadn't filled him in on all the details of their deal.

That was no accident. Most of her crowd wasn't even thinking much about college yet, let alone the rest of their lives. Would Alex think she was weird for being so focused on this deal with her dad?

If he did, maybe it was time to find out. Otherwise what was the point of taking things any further?

"Yeah, I don't think I mentioned it earlier, but I'm actually on kind of a tight schedule with Legs," she said. "See, I'm thinking maybe I want to go pro after I age out of juniors—do horses for a living. My dad's not sure that's such a hot idea. So we made a deal. If I can sell Legs for a profit by the end of the fall shows, he'll think about letting me make a go of it instead of, like, majoring in something boring at Georgetown."

She shot Alex a sidelong glance, trying to gauge his reaction in the milky-dim moonlight. "That's cool," he said, looking thoughtful. "And trust me, I totally understand what you're talking about. My folks want me to go into law or finance or something dull and safe like that."

"And you're not into it?" Tommi guessed.

"No way. My thing's music, you know that already. I want to be, like, a producer or a promoter. Maybe manage a club. Something like that."

"Yeah, that definitely seems more up your alley," Tommi said. They'd spent part of the drive out here listening to his iPod and talking about favorite music, and Tommi had been impressed by his depth of knowledge of bands old and new, popular and obscure.

"Yeah." He shrugged. "Kind of sucks when your family doesn't believe in the dream though, huh?"

"I hear you," Tommi said ruefully. "My dad seems to think my plans are about as serious as me collecting Breyer horses when I was little."

"Forget about that. You'll show him." Alex reached out with his free hand and carefully brushed back a strand of hair that the ocean breeze had just blown into Tommi's eyes. "He'll believe in you then. Hey, that reminds me of that song I was playing for you earlier—it's called 'Believe in Me,' remember?"

Tommi nodded, a little distracted by the lingering warmth on her forehead where his fingers had brushed against her sunburned skin. "I remember. It was one of my favorites," she said.

He smiled, leaning a little closer. "'Believe in me, 'cause I believe in you,'" he sang in a light, husky tenor. "'Believe in us, 'cause our love is true . . .'" Trailing off, he laughed self-consciously. "Okay, now you know why I'm interested in the business end of the music scene or maybe playing guitar or whatever instead of singing."

"No, that was amazing!" Tommi said quickly, squeezing his hand. "Seriously, you have a great voice. I can't remember the last time a guy sang to me."

"I find that hard to believe." He lifted his free hand, running it up her arm, his eyes suddenly intense in the moonlight. "You're the amazing one, Tommi Aaronson."

Tommi held her breath, knowing what was coming. His hand slipped around her shoulder, pulling her toward him. She tipped her head up, letting her eyes fall shut as his lips found hers.

Perfect.

"Easy, *señor*," Miguel murmured to the rangy bay Thoroughbred, who was shifting his weight impatiently at the end of his lead. "You just let Kate rinse you off, and then we'll go for a nice walk and see if we can find some grass, *sí*?"

"Almost done," Kate told the groom, giving the gelding's legs one last blast with the hose. The water pressure at the show grounds wasn't as good as it was at home, but it was good enough. "There, that should do it."

"Good. I'll take him out to dry." Miguel ran a sweat scraper expertly over the horse's body, knocking off most of the water.

"You sure? I can take him if you have other stuff to do."

The groom glanced at her over the horse's back. He was a compact man with broad, strong shoulders and an expression that usually verged on sleepy. But Kate had worked with him long enough to know that his looks were deceiving. Miguel had forgotten more about horses than most people would ever know, and was always willing to share that knowledge. He'd taught Kate as much as Jamie had—maybe more.

"Nope. All caught up," he told Kate with a smile. "We should enjoy it, *sí*? Things will get busy again tomorrow."

Kate glanced around, surprised to realize she was caught up, too. It was Wednesday, early afternoon, and Jamie had just finished riding the Thoroughbred jumper to prep him for his owner, Dani. She was due to arrive tomorrow, along with most of the other juniors and some of the ammys, which meant that what Miguel had said was true—things were about to get a lot busier.

"Oh," Kate said. "I guess you're right."

She'd been running nonstop since getting to the show-grounds on Monday, and it felt weird to suddenly have nothing much to do. Sort of like being on course in a jumper class and not being quite sure which was your next fence.

Miguel clucked to the gelding. "Come on, *amigo*."

"I guess I could sneak in a quick hack on Fable," Kate said, thinking aloud. "Or maybe I should lunge Legs first. He needs to get out of his stall, since Tommi's not here yet to exercise him." She was still a little surprised that her friend had changed her schedule. Tommi took showing more seriously than anyone Kate knew, except maybe Jamie. Especially now that she was prepping Legs for sale.

Miguel stopped and glanced back at her. "Go for your hack," he said. "I'll lunge Legs when I finish with this guy."

"Are you sure?" Kate said. "I mean, I really don't mind doing it, it's just that I haven't even been on Fable since Monday, and—"

"I'm sure," Miguel said. "Go ride!"

"Thanks, Miguel." Kate watched him go, feeling guilty. Still, she reminded herself that her rides on Fable weren't all fun and games. If he did well enough in the eq, he'd fetch a much higher price, which meant a bigger commission for Jamie. That made her feel a little better—like she was earning her keep, not just going on a joyride.

Soon she had the big gray tied in the extra stall used for tacking up. He was in a lively mood, as usual, jumping at each crackle of the PA system and flicking his ears at every passing person, horse, or dog.

"Settle down, you big brute," Kate told him with a laugh as he spooked at a bird in the rafters of the temporary stabling and almost landed on her foot. "Save your energy for the jumps, okay?"

Just then her phone rang. She answered it without looking, assuming it was Jamie or Miguel. But it wasn't.

"Hi, gorgeous," Fitz's familiar voice said into her ear. "Miss me?"

"Fitz!" Kate quickly switched the phone to her other ear, yanking her currycomb out of Fable's reach as he tried to nibble on it. "Um, hi! Where are you?"

"At the barn, where else?" he said. "Things are a little warm at home these days. I still can't believe my parents are making me skip this show!"

Kate didn't respond to that. She always felt a weird little squiggle of guilt when Fitz complained about his punishment for the Ford situation. As if it was all her fault, because he'd done it to impress her.

Not that I asked him to, she reminded herself for the umpteenth time. As usual, that didn't make her feel much better.

"So how are things at Pelham Lane?" she asked. "Quiet?"

"Too quiet," he said. "Plus Joy took the stirrups off both my saddles and hid them somewhere."

Kate laughed at his disgruntled tone. That definitely sounded like Joy. Jamie's assistant trainer was one of those people who was always smiling and never had an unkind word to say about anyone. But she could be just as tough as her boss when someone slacked off or screwed up. Sure, she did it with a smile. But that wouldn't make Fitz's legs ache any less after half a dozen times through a gymnastic stirrupless.

"Just be glad she didn't hide the saddles, too," she teased.

"Ugh! Don't give her any ideas!" he exclaimed in mock horror. "But enough about me. A little stirrupless torture is cake. The worst part about being stuck here is missing you like crazy. So how's the most beautiful girl in the tristate area?"

Kate was almost getting used to his lavish compliments. Still, as she glanced down at herself, horse slobber, baggy schooling breeches, and all, she couldn't help wondering if he was really imagining the right girl.

"I'm fine," she said. "Keeping busy. The usual." Just then Jamie appeared in the stall door. "Listen, Jamie's here. I've got to go. I'll call you later, okay?"

"I'll be sitting by the phone."

As Kate hung up, Jamie stepped in and gave Fable a pat. Chaucer wandered in after him, settling onto his haunches and letting his big pink tongue loll out.

"Everything okay in here?" Jamie asked.

"Sure," Kate said, stepping over to give the bulldog a pat. He was the only one of Jamie's dogs who came to shows, and everyone considered him a sort of barn mascot. "I was just going to go for a short hack. Miguel thought it would be okay—we already raked the aisle, and Miguel's going to lunge Legs—"

"That's fine," Jamie interrupted. "I think it's a good idea. The more you ride him, the more in sync you'll be in the show ring." He paused, peering at her face. "You look tired. Did you eat lunch yet?"

Kate shrugged. "Is it lunchtime already?" she mumbled, realizing that she'd forgotten to eat anything since her toast and OJ early that morning at the hotel.

Jamie chuckled. "You sound like me," he said. "Sit tight, I think I've got something to tide you over until after your ride."

He disappeared, and Kate heard him rummaging around in the tack stall next door. In the meantime she went back to work, setting a fitted fleece pad on Fable's broad back as Chaucer watched.

"Stop that," she told the horse when he shuddered his skin, making the pad slip out of place. "It's a pad, not a fly. I promise."

She replaced the pad and quickly lifted the saddle onto it. As she buckled the girth onto the near-side billets, Jamie reappeared.

"Heads up," he said.

Kate looked up in time to catch what he'd just tossed her. It was a package of peanut butter sandwich cookies.

"I know it's not exactly health food," the trainer said with a smile. "But the sugar rush should get you through the ride at least." He checked his watch. "Speaking of riding, I'm supposed to be getting on Mrs. Walsh's mare right now. See you."

"Bye. Thanks," Kate said, though he was already gone. Jamie never seemed to slow down at the shows—he was always busy riding, coaching, or any of the zillion other tasks he had to do.

Kate set the sandwich cookies on a shelf out of Chaucer's reach so she could finish buckling Fable's girth. She knew better than to leave it half done—the big gray gelding had a mischievous streak, and was likely to dump the saddle on the ground if she gave him half a chance.

After she finished with that, she stepped over and grabbed the package again. Now that she thought about it, she realized she *was* pretty hungry.

She ripped open the package, the strong scents of processed peanut butter and grease making her stomach growl eagerly. Chaucer sidled closer, drool dripping from his jowls.

"Sorry, buddy," Kate told the dog. "This one's for me."

Wiping her hand on her shirt, she grabbed one of the cookies and popped it into her mouth. It actually tasted pretty good, and she glanced at the package in her hand to see how many more there were.

Four. There were a total of four cookies in the package.

Instantly, she flashed to her mother. Four was her magic number—the number that everything had to be arranged into to keep the world from ending. Or whatever it was she thought would happen if she allowed anything in her sight to remain in sets of three, or five, or seventy-nine. If she were here, Kate knew she would have counted the cookies before she ever allowed Kate—or anyone else—to start eating them. If she were the one eating, she'd take exactly four bites to finish each one, and wipe her hands four times to get the grease off.

Kate squeezed her eyes shut, trying to banish the thoughts. But her mind just skittered on without her, trying to figure out whether the total number of saddles in the tack stall next door was divisible by four, exactly how many horses were at the show . . . The half-chewed cookie turned to glue in her mouth.

"Here," she blurted out, tossing the rest of the cookies to Chaucer. Maybe that would make the thoughts stop.

She was shaking as she reached for Fable's bridle. But she tried to ignore it. She didn't have time to be crazy like her mom.

Zara sat slumped on one of the loft's sleek retro-modern sofas, picking at a hangnail and trying to ignore the chaos going on around her. It was Wednesday afternoon, and the whole entourage was flying out to Amsterdam in a couple of hours. Whoop-de-freaking-doo.

One of her father's personal assistants hustled past, carrying an armful of clothes. He stopped short when he noticed her.

"Hey, is the cousin here yet?" he called to Zac's lawyer.

The lawyer didn't bother to look up from his laptop. "S'posed to get here any minute."

Zac sauntered into the room, dressed in snakeskin pants and a jade green velvet smoking jacket. Yeah. Not exactly typical air-travel clothes for most people. But the chartered jet was leaving from JFK, and no way would Zac risk ending up in some passing fan's Photobucket album looking less than rock-star fabulous. No surprise there. He put on eyeliner to walk to the bagel shop on the corner.

"Hanging in, Little Z?" he asked, wandering toward her with an unlit cigarette hanging from his lip. He'd banned himself from smoking in the loft, claiming he was trying to quit.

Yeah, right. He'd been saying that for as long as Zara could remember. Come to think of it, she'd never noticed him ever actually *trying*, at least not when her mom wasn't around.

"Whatever," she said with a frown. "I'm supposed to sit here and wait for Nanny Dearest to get here, so that's what I'm doing. Happy?"

"Ecstatic." The corner of Zac's mouth twitched with amusement. He was always in a good mood when he was about to go on tour.

No wonder. Zara glanced around the loft. Everyone else had to do all the work, and he just got to enjoy the good stuff.

As Zac went over to talk to his bassist, who was sprawled out on the floor nearby reading a motorcycle magazine, Zara stood and stretched. Then she padded over to the window in her bare feet. She was still in the shorts and tank top she'd slept in, having only woken up an hour earlier thanks to hanging out with some new acquaintances at some lame coffeehouse until like 5:00 a.m. Kind of boring, but she'd been making a point. Not that Zac had even noticed. He'd been asleep way before she got home, resting up for the big trip.

Then she smiled as she remembered one not-boring part about last night. That cute friend of Tommi's, Grant. He'd called around nine, wanting to get together sometime.

Zac's lawyer glanced up as she wandered past him. "What?" he demanded, looking harried.

"Nothing. Can't I walk around my own house?" Zara retorted. "Or aren't I allowed to move without my babysitter's permission?"

The guy had already turned his attention back to his computer. "Save the pity party for someone who cares, Zara," he muttered.

Zara scowled. Who the hell did this pointy-headed loser

think he was, anyway? But before she could muster up enough energy to react, the buzzer sounded.

"That must be Cousin Stacie," Zac called to her. "Come on over and help me welcome her."

"Do I have to?" Zara muttered.

Zac ignored her, striding toward the door. One of the guys had already hit the button to buzz the visitor in, and within minutes she was there.

Cousin Stacie was pretty much what Zara had expected. Blond ponytail. Tidy khaki shorts and a polo shirt. Uptight expression. The works.

"Hi, Cousin Zac!" Stacie exclaimed in a voice just as perky as her ponytail. "It's so awesome to finally meet you! My mom's always telling stories about all the trouble you guys got up to when you were kids."

Zac chuckled. "Don't believe a word of it, darlin'," he said with a wink. "Your mom's always been one for tall tales."

Zara rolled her eyes. Stacie turned just in time to see, though her expression didn't change.

"And you must be Zara," she said.

"I guess I must," Zara said.

Zac shot her a warning look. "Easy, Little Z," he said. "I'm sure you and Stacie will get along just fine once you get to know each other." He turned to Stacie with a wry smile. "She seems to think I'm being unreasonable by not letting her stay all alone at age sixteen."

Stacie chuckled. "Hey, that's totally normal. At sixteen, I thought I was ready for anything, too."

Okay, Zara *so* wasn't going to stand around and listen to

this. Who did this Stacie chick think she was? At best, she might be four or five years older than Zara. And had probably seen way less of the world, growing up in Upper Dipshit County out in the middle of nowhere.

"Excuse me," Zara said. "I've got stuff to do."

"Hey, Little Z!" Zac called after her.

Zara didn't even slow down, taking the stairs two at a time and slamming her bedroom door behind her.

She spent the next hour in her room, lying on her bed listening to music and waiting for someone to come check on her. But nobody showed until almost five, when Mickey knocked at the door.

"Gettin' ready to leave, sweetheart," he said in his raspy voice. "Your dad wants you to come down and say good-bye."

Zara thought about refusing. If it had been anyone else asking, she probably would have. But she liked Mickey—he was her favorite member of the posse—and so she climbed to her feet.

"Whatever," she muttered. "Let's go."

Cousin Stacie was watching as the bodyguards hauled the last of the luggage out of the apartment. She turned as Zara plodded down the steps, but didn't say a word.

"There you are." Zac sounded distracted as he hurried over. "We're off. All the digits and schedule and crap are written down in the message center, so just call if you need anything." He bent and planted a quick kiss on her curly dark hair. "Don't do anything I wouldn't do while I'm gone, okay?"

"How can I?" Zara shot a sour look toward Stacie.

Zac ignored that. Or maybe he hadn't even heard it. Zara couldn't tell.

"Ready, guys?" he shouted with a grin. "Let's motor!"

The remaining posse members let out a whoop. Moments later, they were all gone.

Zara walked over to the window to watch the line of limos and vans pull away from the curb. When they'd disappeared around the corner onto Broome Street, she turned away. Stacie was standing there, staring at her.

"Listen," Stacie said. "I think we should sit down and have a little talk about how the next few weeks are going to work."

"Maybe some other time. I've got a really ugly headache all of a sudden." Zara headed back upstairs, ignoring Stacie's tentative calls.

Zara locked herself in her room, then flopped onto her bed and pulled out her phone. No way was she hanging around here with Stacie Poppins bossing her around. No. Way.

"Zara? Hi!" Grant sounded pleased when he picked up the phone. "What's up?"

"Was just going to ask you the same thing," Zara said. Tucking the phone between her head and shoulder, she wandered over to the mirror to see how much work she had to do to make herself look presentable. "You doing anything? 'Cause I'm bored. Want to hang out?"

"You mean right now?"

She smiled at the note of surprise in his voice. Yeah, it was pretty obvious this guy was used to hanging out with girls like Tommi. Girls who expected to make plans ahead of time, and who probably wouldn't even let a guy hold her hand on the first date, let alone anything more.

"Hell yeah, right now," she said. "You got something better going on?"

"No, now's great," he said. "Just tell me where to meet you."

A few minutes later, dressed in her best sexy-slinky clubwear, Zara stepped to the edge of the landing overlooking the first floor. Stacie was nowhere in sight. A second later Zara heard the ice maker in the kitchen clunk.

Good. Maybe she'd get away clean.

She hurried down the stairs. Just as she closed the front door behind her, she heard Stacie calling her name.

But she ignored it. Maybe now Cousin Stacie would get the hint about exactly how these next few weeks were *really* going to work.

FIVE

Tommi stepped to the end of the diving board, bounced once on the balls of her feet, then sliced cleanly into the sun-warmed water. She kicked a couple of times to propel herself forward, then surfaced, reaching up automatically to push back her wet brown shoulder-length hair.

Alex watched from one of the teak lounge chairs as she hoisted herself out of the water and reached for a towel. They were the only two still hanging out by the free-form pool overlooking the beach. It was almost six, and everyone else had gone inside to get changed for dinner.

It had been a hot day and hadn't cooled off much yet, so Tommi wrapped the towel around her waist, leaving her upper body and Luli Fama bikini top to air dry. Then she grabbed her watch, which she'd left on a table.

She groaned when she saw how late it was. "I can't believe it's time to go already."

"So don't go." Alex reached up, grabbed her hand, and pulled her onto the lounge beside him. "Stay one more day."

"I wish I could." Tommi smiled at him. His hair had dried in funny little peaks, making him look impish and adorable. "But I'm showing tomorrow, remember?"

"Yeah, I know." He reached out and pushed a stray strand of wet hair out of her eyes. "And showing's important to you, and there's the whole Legs thing with your dad. I totally get that. It's just been so cool getting to know you, I wish you could hang out a little longer."

"Me too," Tommi said, meaning it. The past two days had been amazing. That incredible kiss on the beach the first night hadn't been a fluke, and neither had the great time they'd had together on the drive out. Alex was everything she liked in a guy—smart, funny, ambitious, a little snarky, and totally into her. He even still seemed interested in hearing about the horse stuff, which was more than Tommi could say for most of the guys she knew.

For some reason, thinking about that reminded her of Grant. To be fair, he'd shown at least a little bit of interest in horses. He'd even come to a couple of shows to watch her ride. But that was different. Anyway, she couldn't help being relieved that he'd had to miss this house party due to a doctor's appointment and a family party. Otherwise things could've been pretty awkward.

She forgot about Grant as Alex scooted closer. "Sure you can't give this show a pass? Just this once?" he wheedled.

"I can't. Seriously." Tommi smiled, flattered that he was trying so hard to change her mind even as she mentally calculated how long it would take her to drive back to the city. "For one thing, I promised this girl Zara from my barn I'd drive her down there tomorrow. She's kind of counting on me for a ride."

"Zara?" he echoed. "Wait, why does that name sound familiar? Did you mention her before?"

"Maybe. I don't know." Tommi shrugged. She'd talked a lot about the barn, though she couldn't remember if Zara had come up. "She only moved to the barn earlier this summer. Before that she rode in LA—she's the daughter of Zac Trask and Gina Girard."

Alex sat up straight. "Zac Trask?" he said. "As in the singer Zac Trask? Seriously?"

"Yeah, that's the one, fanboy." Tommi couldn't help smiling at his reaction. "Want me to get his autograph for you?"

Alex laughed. "Sorry, yeah, guess that came out a little geeky," he said. "It's just, you know, *Zac Trask*. Actually though, I met him this one time last summer at a party over in Amagansett. Seemed like a cool guy."

"I guess." Tommi's eyes wandered to her watch. "I've only met him once myself. But listen, I really should get going soon, or—"

"Yo, lovebirds!" Duckface came out onto the back deck and waved at them. "We're taking a vote. Indian food or Thai?"

"I could go either way," Alex said. He glanced at Tommi. "What about you? The new Thai place is really good. And you've got to eat, right?"

"Yeah, but I've got to sleep, too," Tommi said, laughing as he tugged on her arm, pulling her to her feet and toward the house. "And if I stay here for dinner, I won't get home until way late."

"Pretty please? For me?" He stopped and faced her, smiling hopefully.

She hesitated, knowing she should stay firm. That would be the responsible thing to do, the adult thing. But looking into his eyes, remembering how much fun they'd been having, she couldn't make herself do it.

"Well . . . I guess I do have to eat," she said.

"Woo-hoo!" Alex grabbed her in an impulsive hug that turned into a kiss. Tommi didn't even remember that Duck-face was still outside until she heard him let out a wolf whistle. She pulled her face away from Alex's, both of them laughing.

"Come on," Tommi said. "Let's go in and vote."

The two of them strolled into the house hand in hand to join the debate about where to eat. Tommi was trying to enjoy the feeling—this tentative-new-couple stage was one of her favorite parts of a relationship. But she was distracted by the sense of time passing. Tick-tock, tick-tock. Every minute that went by was one less she would get to sleep tonight.

"Tommi?" Courtney waved her hand in front of Tommi's face. "Wake up. You're the deciding vote."

"Huh?" Tommi blinked, realizing she'd spaced out while the others were talking. "Oh. Um, Thai sounds good."

Half the crowd cheered, while the rest groaned or cussed her out playfully. Alex leaned closer and planted a kiss on her cheek.

"Excellent choice, Miss Aaronson," he said.

"Thanks, Mr. Nakano." She smiled at him, suddenly annoyed with herself for stressing out over something so stupid. What was the big deal? She was young and enjoying life. A little lost sleep shouldn't even be on her radar.

"Easy, tiger," Zara murmured as she felt Grant's hand slip inside her clothes. "We don't want to put on a show for the driver."

"Why stop now?" The cabbie, a skinny guy with an Eastern European accent and a sarcastic streak, glanced at them in the rearview. "I was about to start filming this for YouTube."

"We're paying you to drive, not to crack lame jokes," Zara reminded him. She glanced out the window, forcing her eyes to focus until the dancing, swirling lights settled down into their normal patterns and she could see that they were only a couple of blocks from the loft. Wow, how many drinks had she had, anyway?

Not as many as Grant, at least. The boy was seriously drunk. He was already groping at her again, mumbling a bunch of crap about how she made him feel. If only his prep school friends could see him now! She smiled at the thought.

"So tonight was fun," she said, grabbing the armrest as the cab swerved around a stopped car. The driver leaned out the open window and let out a torrent of curses in whatever language he spoke.

"Yeah, it was great," Grant slurred, clumsily running his hand up her leg. "I've never met anyone like you, Zara."

"I'll bet you haven't." She smirked, feeling good about how the evening had gone. Grant was sweet, and she just loved corrupting a sweet guy.

"Here we are, young lovers," the cabbie announced, skidding to a stop in front of the loft. "Now get out of my cab before I have to disinfect it."

"Give it a rest, dude," Zara said. "Listen, make sure this guy gets home, okay?" She gave him Grant's Upper East Side address, hoping she was remembering it right. But whatever—guys like Grant always landed on their feet, right? "Trust me, he's got the cash to pay when you get there."

"Whatever." The cabbie shrugged, turning up the radio.

Grant seemed to clue in to what was going on. He grabbed Zara, turning her to face him. "Wait. When will I see you again?" he asked.

Instead of answering, she grabbed him for a good-night kiss. He cradled her face with one hand and her ass with the other, bending her back against the car door. Zara put everything she had into it—drunk or not, she wanted him to remember this. Then the cabbie started muttering under his breath and Zara pulled back, straightening her skirt.

"I'll call you, okay?" she said. "See you."

She hopped out of the taxi before he could respond, slamming the door shut. A second later the cab peeled away and sped down the street.

Zara swayed a little, catching her balance on her high heels. Okay, yeah, she was definitely a little drunk. But whatever. She could handle it.

She staggered into the elevator and hit the button for the top floor, wondering what Nanny Stacie was going to say when she walked in. Actually, she was sort of surprised some kind of NYPD missing-persons squad hadn't been waiting for her outside the building. Stacie totally seemed like the type to panic and call in the cavalry.

The elevator slid open, spitting Zara out onto the landing. Wow, her head was really pounding. Or *was* that her head?

She blinked, realizing there was music coming from behind the loft door. Loud music.

"Huh?" she muttered, fumbling for her key.

When she let herself in, the first thing she saw was a buff guy in his early twenties dancing in the middle of the room with his shirt off. And his pants, too, actually. All he had on was a pair of silk boxers.

Then she looked around and saw three other guys she'd never seen before. One was sucking down a beer and playing Grand Theft Auto on the plasma TV. Another was digging through Zac's liquor cabinet. The third was on the couch with his tongue stuck down Zara's cousin's throat.

"Hey!" Zara said loudly. "What's going on?"

"Zara! You're home!" Stacie shoved the guy away. "Dude, people in New York are, like, sooo friendly!" She giggled as the guy grabbed her and nibbled at her earlobe. "Quit it! I mean it!"

She pushed him away again and stood. The khaki shorts and dorky polo were gone; Stacie was now dressed in a sparkly cami and a skirt even shorter and tighter than Zara's.

"Listen," she said, her voice sounding kind of melted around the edges. Even in her own condition, Zara could tell the girl was wasted. "Sorry about earlier, okay? I was just, you know, giving Cousin Zac what I figured he wanted to see, you know? We cool?"

Zara just stared at her cousin for a second. Her babysitter. The person who was supposed to keep her out of trouble. Then a smile spread across her face as she got it.

"Yeah," she said. "We're so totally cool."

Kate yawned, then checked her watch. One thirty a.m. The showgrounds had cleared out hours ago except for their little corner of the temporary stalls. All the lights were on in their aisles, and Kate, Miguel, and Max were slumped on a bench right outside the tack stall.

Jamie appeared at the end of the aisle, leading an exhausted-looking liver chestnut gelding, a children's hunter belonging to one of the younger girls in the barn. Miguel climbed to his feet. "I'll take the next turn," he offered.

"Thanks." Jamie handed over the lead. For once, he looked less than perfectly groomed. His shirt was untucked, his normally flawless dark hair rumpled.

Kate was sure she looked just as bad. They all did. A colicky horse could do that to you.

"Is he any better?" she asked Jamie as Miguel disappeared with the horse.

"Still no poop." Jamie stifled a yawn and leaned against the wall. "But listen, you should probably head back to the hotel—you too," he added, glancing at Max. "No sense all of us staying up all night. Miguel and I can handle it."

Kate shook her head. "I'm not that tired," she lied. "Besides, I want to help."

Colic was the catchall name for equine stomach troubles, and the bane of a horseman's existence. This particular horse had a history of minor gas colics, and usually recovered quickly. But this time the vet had come and gone, tubing with mineral oil to try to clear out a possible impaction, and still the gelding hadn't passed any manure. Kate knew there wasn't much point in trying to sleep. Not until she knew that the horse was going to be okay.

"I'll stay too, boss," Max put in. He stood up, stretching. "Might as well muck stalls while I wait my turn."

Kate nodded. "And I never did get around to organizing the meds trunk," she said. "Think I'll take care of that now."

Soon she was straightening vials of Banamine, Robaxin, and all the other drugs that kept the hardworking show horses happy and sound. But she wasn't really seeing them. She was worrying about what might happen next. What if it wasn't just a gas colic this time, but a twist or serious impaction? What if the horse crashed right here, thrashing so wildly from the pain in its belly that it made things even worse? What if it died in front of them, before they could even get it to a clinic for surgery?

Those kinds of thoughts made her feel helpless and edgy. Sure, all the horses in Jamie's barn were insured, and even if they hadn't been, most of the owners could pay the thousands of dollars for colic surgery without blinking an eye. But sometimes even money wasn't enough. Horses seemed so big and strong most of the time, but then there were times like these when they reminded you just how fragile they really were. How quickly things could go wrong, and how little humans could do about it.

Kate had finished the meds cabinet and moved on to tidying the supplements tub when she heard a happy shout from outside. Dropping the bucket of electrolytes she'd been holding, she hurried into the aisle.

"What?" she asked.

Miguel turned and grinned at her from his position at the chestnut gelding's head. "We have poop!" he announced.

"Thank God!" Kate exclaimed. She hurried over to pat the horse, who already looked a little perkier as he nosed at a stray piece of hay on the ground. "You had us worried, buddy."

"Only in a barn could a bunch of sane people get so excited about horse poop," Jamie joked wearily.

"Sane? Says who?" Max retorted with a smirk.

Jamie chuckled. "Okay, now it really is time to go get some rest. Miguel's going to sleep in the barn just in case. I'll give you two a ride to the hotel."

"Thanks." Kate gave the horse one last pat, said good night to Miguel, then followed Jamie and Max toward the parking lot, trying not to count the short hours until it was time to get up and do it all again.

SIX

—   —   —   —   —

Zara awoke to an insistent, annoying buzzing sound. She slapped at her alarm clock, knocking it to the floor. But the sound persisted.

BZZZZZZZZ!

"Shut the hell up!" Zara mumbled into her pillow.

Her head was pounding too much to lift it, so she just rolled over and cracked an eye open, staring at the ceiling.

BZZZZZZZZ!

Doorbell. That's what it was, she realized.

"Isn't anyone going to answer that?" she yelled hoarsely.

No answer. The loft was silent except for that annoying buzzer.

That's when she remembered. Zac and the rest of them were gone. There were no roadies or toadies around to do stuff like answer the door. That meant the brain-splitting noise probably wasn't going to stop until she got up and took care of it herself.

She climbed to her feet, muttering every curse word she could think of under her breath. Her head was already clearing a little, and she realized it was still pretty early—barely 7:00 a.m.

"Who would be here at the freaking crack of dawn?" she complained as she reached the bottom of the stairs and stumbled over a wadded-up T-shirt. Mr. Half Naked must've left it behind last night.

Swallowing a yawn, she swung open the door. Tommi was standing there, looking kind of cranky.

"Are you kidding me?" Tommi snapped. "You're not even dressed!"

Zara glanced down at herself. She barely remembered changing into her pj's after downing a few more drinks with Stacie and her new friends.

"Oops," she said. "Today's the day we're supposed to leave for the show, isn't it?"

Just then a door swung open upstairs. "What's going on?" Stacie called blearily, leaning over the railing wrapped in a short pink terry-cloth robe. She looked about like Zara felt.

"It's nothing," Zara called. "Just someone here to pick me up for my show."

"Your what?" Stacie blinked, looking confused.

Tommi blew out a loud, impatient sigh. "Just what I need this morning," she announced to nobody in particular. She shot a glare at Zara. "Look, I'm going across the street for coffee. Be out by my car in twenty minutes, or I'm leaving without you."

"Whatever," Zara said as Tommi stomped off toward the elevator.

"Whoa," Stacie said, stumbling down the staircase. "Who was that chick? Uptight much?"

Zara yawned and swung the door shut. "Nobody," she said. "I mean, she's just my ride to this show, like I said. I sort of made plans for her to pick me up here."

"Oh." Stacie wandered over to the coffee table. A half-full glass of amber liquid was sitting there, and she sniffed at it, took a sip, then set it down again. "So that means I don't have to drive you anywhere for the next few days?"

"Yeah, in theory," Zara said. Part of the deal with Zac was that Stacie was supposed to be her ride to the barn and anywhere else she needed to go. "I'm thinking I might ditch the show, though. Tell Jamie I'm sick or something."

"What?" That actually seemed to wake Stacie up a little. "Wait, no. You should totally go."

"Why? You trying to get rid of me already?"

Stacie pushed a chunk of tangled blond hair behind her ear. "Nothing personal, okay? It's just that, you know, I wouldn't mind some alone time with Tad."

"Tad? Who the hell's Tad?" Then Zara figured it out. "You mean that loser guy from last night?"

Stacie's sheepish grin gave her the answer. Zara rolled her eyes.

At first she was ready to tell Stacie tough shit. She was hungover, she'd barely gotten any sleep, and she wasn't in the mood to do anyone any favors. Besides, how annoying was it that her brand-new country cousin was already trying to ditch her? This was her house, for crap's sake!

But she held off. As she woke up a little more, she realized she couldn't blow off this show. She was still on probation with Jamie for the time she'd been caught smoking in the barn. She couldn't risk pissing him off right now.

"Don't worry, you'll have the place to yourself soon," she said with a sigh. "I just need to shower and find my . . . Damn!"

"What?" Stacie flopped onto the sofa and yawned.

"I just remembered I never got my show clothes cleaned after Hounds Hollow," Zara said. "Usually I get one of the guys to send them out, but everything was so crazy around here last week, I sort of forgot. Last time I saw them, they were in a corner of my closet floor."

Stacie shoved an empty tequila bottle aside with her big toe so she could prop her legs up on the coffee table. "Don't you have any other clothes you can wear besides the dirty ones?" she asked. "I thought Cousin Zac was loaded."

"Yeah, I have other stuff I could wear."

For a moment Zara considered doing just that. Last year's jackets still fit her and would do, even if they weren't the most current style. Ditto for breeches. And of course she had about a million show shirts.

Then she had a better idea. "No biggie," she said with a smile. "I'll just pick up something new at the vendors when I get there."

"Vendors?" Stacie wrinkled her nose, looking confused.

"At the show. They're these, like, traveling shops or what-ever. They sell tack, clothes, helmets, all kinds of crap. Sure, it might be a little more expensive." She shrugged. "But what the hell? Zac's loaded, right?"

Zara smiled, picturing what Nerdy Accountant Guy would

say when he saw that credit card statement. Served Zac right for sticking her with a stupid babysitter, even if she hadn't turned out to be as bad as Zara had expected.

Suddenly realizing that several minutes had already passed, Zara knew she needed to hustle. She should have just enough time to jump in the shower and find her boots before Tommi's deadline.

🐎

Elliot stuck his head into the empty stall Kate was mucking out. "I'm going to get food," the groom said. "Want something?"

Kate straightened up and leaned on her manure fork. "Sure, thanks," she said. "Maybe a burger, or whatever looks fast and easy? I don't have much time before I have to start getting horses ready for the pre-green warm-up."

"One burger it is." Elliot smiled, then disappeared.

Kate finished the stall, then headed out into the aisle herself, stifling a yawn. It was only a little after one, and her lack of sleep last night was already catching up with her. Even after returning to the hotel, she'd had trouble turning off her brain after that colic scare. She'd just kept running the whole scenario through her head, imagining all the what-ifs and could-have-beens. In the end, she figured she was lucky if she'd gotten a couple of hours of real sleep.

"Kate!" a loud, no-nonsense voice broke her out of her sleepy thoughts. "Thank God. Are you busy right now?"

Turning her head, Kate saw Jamie's adult client Margie O'Donnell hurrying toward her. The woman was scheduled to ride in the Level 4 Jumpers in a few hours and was already half dressed for it in rolled-up show breeches paired with flip-flops and a tank top. That was par for the course. Margie was one of those people who didn't care what anyone else thought about her.

In any case, Kate didn't bother to tell Margie that she was pretty much *always* busy on show days. "What's up?" she asked instead.

Margie waved her tricked-out BlackBerry, which she never went anywhere without, and launched into an obscenity-laden complaint about her office and some big project. Kate's brain wasn't functioning well enough to follow most of it.

"Um, so you have to leave the show?" she asked.

"Hell no! I'm not letting those freaking bozos ruin my week-end." Margie made a face. "But I was just about to get Lark out, and now I'm going to have to go deal with this . . ."

Now Kate understood. Margie had one of the craziest work schedules of anyone at the barn, but she still liked doing as much hands-on care of her horses as she could manage. She especially liked being the one to hand graze her jumper mare, Larkspur, who got antsy being cooped up in a small show stall for too long.

"You want me to take her out for a while?" Kate asked, shoving her half-full wheelbarrow against the wall so it would be out of the way. "No problem, I'll go get her right now."

"Kate, you're a freaking saint," Margie said gratefully. "Thanks a million. I'll have you to thank for not getting bucked off over the first warm-up jump this afternoon."

Shooting Kate one last smile, she pressed her phone to her ear and stalked off, muttering under her breath about her coworkers. Kate turned the other way and headed toward Lark's stall.

On her way, she passed Elliot. "Cancel that burger," she told him. "I've got to graze Margie's mare."

"You sure?" the groom said.

Kate nodded. "Horse show burgers are gross enough when they're warm," she joked. "I don't even want to think about eating a cold one. I'll grab something later."

Soon she was out in a grassy spot near the back gate with a compact bay horse at the end of the lead. The mare was a spitfire, which made her a perfect match for Margie, who was one of Jamie's gutsiest and most competitive adults. At the moment, though, Lark seemed content to graze quietly like a lazy school pony.

That was fine with Kate. She yawned and switched the lead to her other hand. It already felt like she was sleepwalking through this day, and the hot summer sun blazing down on her wasn't helping. Her mind drifted back to last night's colic scare. The liver chestnut gelding seemed fine today, though his owner had scratched all their classes this weekend at Jamie's advice.

Kate let the lead slip a little farther through her hand as Lark stretched for an extra-tasty patch of clover. Even though she was staring right at the horse, Kate's mind was still elsewhere, and it took her a moment to react when she saw Lark take a step to the side, one steel-shod hoof landing squarely on the lead rope, pinning it to the ground.

Before Kate could react, or even really take in what was happening, the horse tried to lift her head and grunted in surprise as she hit the end of the lead. Planting both feet, Lark jerked back, her eyes wide with panic.

"No!" Kate blurted out. Her mind was still working in slow motion. She watched as Lark hit the end of the rope again, this time with all the force of the thousand-plus-pound horse's panic behind it. The halter's thin leather crown strap broke, as it was designed to do, and the whole thing slid off over Lark's nose, leaving her head bare.

The mare still looked panicky, not quite sure if she was really free, if the monster that had momentarily grabbed her head was really gone. She tossed her head and skittered backward, almost bumping into Kate, then spun and squealed. Kate clutched the lead now hanging uselessly in her hand, realizing there was nothing keeping the mare from running off.

"Easy, girl!" Kate took a slow step forward, trying to keep the panic out of her voice. "It's okay, baby."

Lark jigged in place, her ears flicking back and forth. Kate could tell by the horse's body language that she wasn't sure what to do. Freeze, or run? Kate tried not to imagine what would happen if she chose the latter. If Lark bolted in one direction, she'd end up running through the stables, possibly crashing into a horse cross-tied in the aisle or trampling whoever was in her way. The other direction, and she'd be heading straight for the ring where the baby green hunters were warming up. Jamie was riding a customer's new greenie in that, and Kate could only imagine what he'd think if he saw one of his horses galloping around, leaving chaos in her wake.

"Easy," she said again, her voice shaking a little. The mare was still prancing in place and staring around wild-eyed, but now one ear was cocked in Kate's direction. She was listening. Good. "Just stay there, baby girl," Kate crooned, edging closer.

Finally she was able to get a hand on the mare's neck—and a moment later slide the lead around it.

"Okay, sweetie," she said. "Let's just get you back to your stall, okay?" Giving a gentle tug on the two ends of the lead now looped around the mare's neck, she was relieved when Lark lowered her head and stepped off after her.

Kate didn't stop shaking until Lark was safely back in her stall. That had been a close one, though fortunately it had ended with no real harm done except to the halter. How could she have slacked off like that? She knew how dangerous it could be to let your guard down, especially around fit horses at a busy show. Sure, accidents could happen anywhere when you were dealing with half-ton prey animals, but that kind of carelessness was inexcusable. No matter how tired she was, she had to stay in control.

She went to the tack stall to fetch a new halter and found Tommi just coming out. "Hi," Kate greeted her. "Did you just get here?"

"Little while ago." Tommi sounded irritated. "We were late, thanks to Little Miss Party Girl."

"You mean Zara?" Kate vaguely remembered that the two of them were supposed to drive up together.

"Who else?" Tommi snorted. "I mean, I had a late night, too. And somehow I managed to get myself out of bed and dressed on time. Is it really too much to ask for her to do the same?"

Kate was pretty sure Tommi wasn't expecting an answer to that. Sure enough, she barely paused for breath before launching into the details about her own late night. Something about traffic on the Long Island Expressway and dinner in the Hamptons with that cute new guy she'd mentioned a few times.

Kate did her best to look interested and smile or nod at the right spots, but she couldn't really muster up much enthusiasm. She felt sort of guilty about that—after all, Tommi was supposed to be one of her best friends. But she tried not to worry about it. All she had to do was make it through the rest of the day and get some sleep tonight. Then everything would be fine.

SEVEN

— — — — —

"Ready, boy?" Tommi straightened the noseband on Legs's bridle. "Let's go do this."

She felt her stomach clench, the tuna wrap she'd had for lunch briefly threatening to make a second appearance. Show nerves. They were always there, even if most people thought she was made of steel.

But today was worse than usual. She felt as anxious as a walk-trotter at her first show. And she knew exactly why. For one thing, she was still overtired—she'd stayed out in the Hamptons way too late Wednesday night and was still playing catch-up now, two days later.

For another thing, she could already tell that Legs was wired. And no wonder. The grooms had been lungeing him daily since arriving at the show, but Tommi knew that wasn't really enough for a smart, sensitive horse like Legs. That was why she'd originally planned to do that schooling class on Wednesday. Work the kinks out when there weren't so many people around watching.

Too late now. Tommi wasn't the type to dwell, so she did her best to let it go. They'd have to do their best today and take it from there.

The warm-up ring was chaotic, as always. A few people from the barn were leaning on the fence watching, including Summer. She hurried over when she spotted Tommi coming.

"Hi, Tommi," Summer said. "Want me to hold Legs while you mount?"

"No thanks, I've got it covered." Tommi grabbed a chunk of mane and swung up into the saddle. Legs danced in place, trying to spurt forward as she picked up her stirrups. Yeah, he was amped, all right.

"Jamie's over there." Summer gestured toward the center of the crowded ring. "He just started warming up Dani and Zara. They're the only ones doing the High Juniors today except you, since Fitz isn't here."

"Thanks." Tommi entered the ring and rode over to Jamie, who was standing beside a blue-and-white-striped vertical.

"Tommi," he said, shooting her a look. "Sit tight for a sec, I need to talk to you."

"Okay." Tommi knew that Legs was in no mood to stand still, so she started walking him in a circle as Jamie turned back to the fence.

Zara was approaching it on her jumper, Keeper. The big chestnut was a real pro, and Tommi couldn't help admiring the way he set himself up for the jump, clearing it as easily as if it were no bigger than a crossrail.

"Nice!" Jamie called. "Take him around at a trot for a few minutes." Then he waved to Tommi.

She walked her horse over, wondering what was up. He didn't keep her in the dark for long.

"You know Kara Parodi, right?" he said.

"Sure." Everyone knew Kara Parodi, at least by reputation. She was the head trainer at a big show barn in New Jersey.

Jamie's blue eyes flicked over toward the rail. "Was just talking to her," he said. "She's got a client looking for a scopey young jumper. Says the woman's a good, gutsy rider who doesn't mind a horse with some attitude. She heard about Legs here and thought he might fit the bill. She'll be watching him go today, seeing if he's worth bringing her client for a test ride."

"Really?" Tommi was a little surprised that word was getting around so fast. "That's great!"

But her excitement was tempered with anxiety. She was glad this was happening. But why did it have to happen the one time she'd skipped her warm-up division?

She tried to hide her misgivings. Jamie had already turned away, anyway. He was watching Dani canter toward the warm-up jump. Her horse came in a little fast and flat, but managed to make it over with only a hard rub.

"Let him stop there," Jamie called to Dani. "It looks like he's getting frazzled."

"He is," Dani said breathlessly as her horse skidded to a stop beside Legs. "I think he's having a racetrack flashback or something."

Dani's horse was a Thoroughbred ex-racer, and he could be a pistol. Luckily that suited Dani just fine. She had always been a lot more comfortable in the jumpers than in the hunters.

"He's feeling good today," Dani told Tommi, patting her horse. "A little *too* good, maybe."

Tommi smiled briefly, then glanced over at Jamie, who was fiddling with the warm-up fence. What did he think about her decision to skip out on that Wednesday class? He hadn't really said anything when she'd told him. Then again, she hadn't really asked for his opinion.

Just then Zara rode over to join them. "Hey, girls," Zara sang out. "Ready to watch me and Keeper beat the breeches off all the rest of you in this class?"

"In your dreams, Trask," Dani said with a laugh. "That blue ribbon is mine. Deal with it."

Zara grinned, then glanced over at Tommi. "What about you? You ready to fight Dani for second place, or what?"

"Whatever." Tommi rolled her eyes. She wasn't usually one to hold a grudge, but she was still a little pissed off at Zara for keeping her waiting yesterday. Way to thank her for doing her a favor.

"Oh, so you admit it?" Zara grinned and patted her horse. "Hear that, Keeper? At least these East Coast princesses know when they're in over their heads."

"Who you callin' princess, princess?" Dani joked.

But Tommi just muttered something about starting her warm-up, then turned Legs away from the other two. She wasn't in the mood for trash talking. She had more important things on her mind. Besides, she was better off just keeping quiet and then putting Zara in her place where it counted—in the show ring. After yesterday morning, that would be pretty satisfying, actually.

She sent Legs into a trot to loosen up. Weaving expertly in and out among the warm-up bedlam, she finally found an open spot on the rail and pushed him forward. He opened up his stride willingly, as always. But Tommi frowned slightly. Had she just felt something—a tiny hitch in his step?

She pushed harder, seeing if he'd work out of it. After all, he'd spent a lot more time than usual in a stall lately. No wonder if he was a little stiff.

But even after a good five minutes, that little . . . *something* . . . was still there. Not all the time, not every stride or even every five strides. But often enough for Tommi to feel that something wasn't quite right. She shot a look at the rail. Kara Parodi was over there, watching. Could she see it?

Jamie was talking to the other two girls about the course. Tommi rode over and told him what was going on. He looked concerned.

"Let me see," he said.

Tommi trotted several circles around him. "It's just every once in a while," she said. "Sort of a tiny hesitation, or something. Might be in his hind end—stifles, maybe?"

Jamie watched intently, but finally shrugged. "Sorry, I can't see anything," he said. "Are you sure he's not just tense?"

Tommi bit her lip and shot another look at the rail, where the other trainer was still watching. She wasn't the only one, either. Zara and Dani were both staring curiously.

Now what? Tommi was tempted to trust Jamie's eye, just go ahead and ride the class. The trouble was, she couldn't deny what she felt. She knew Legs pretty well by now, and she knew something wasn't right with him today. It wasn't worth risking his soundness just for one class.

"Sorry," she said slowly. "I think maybe I'd better scratch. I don't want to take any chances."

Jamie was silent for a moment, then nodded. "All right. If you think that's what's best. I'll go tell Kara."

He strode toward the rail as Tommi rode toward the gate. "Never mind, bud," she whispered, giving Legs a pat. "We'll get 'em next time."

She tried not to overhear Jamie giving the other trainer the news, but Parodi wasn't exactly a shrinking violet. The woman's voice carried, and Tommi couldn't help catching some of her annoyed reaction. Something about rich amateurs playing pro.

Yeah, that stung. But Tommi was careful not to let it show.

"Hey!" Zara called, catching up to her right before the gate. "What happened? Sorry, didn't mean to make you choke."

Tommi knew she was only joking. But she *so* wasn't in the mood.

"As if," she said icily, then steered Legs out of the ring without looking back.

Zara leaned on the rail and stared at the overfed bay warmblood loping along at a snail's pace and heaving itself over tiny fences. Adult hunters. Talk about boring.

She turned and wandered away toward the temporary stalls. It was Saturday, and the show was going well so far. She and Keeper had come in fourth in the Junior Jumpers yesterday, beating out Dani, who'd pinned sixth. Too bad Tommi had scratched. It would've been fun to beat her, too, especially after how snotty she'd been about Zara oversleeping.

Oh, well. Maybe next show. Zara was in too good a mood to worry about it. She and Ellie had done well in their hunter rounds earlier today. Now she was just hanging out, waiting for the hack. Unfortunately there wasn't much going on at the moment aside from those boring pre-adult hunters. The grounds crew was setting up the Big Eq course in one ring, some ponies were milling around getting ready to hack in another, and that was pretty much it.

When she reached Pelham Lane's stalls, the only person around was Kate. She was making like a busy little bee, as always, rushing toward the tack stall with an armful of saddle pads.

"Where is everybody?" Zara asked.

Kate blinked, staring around the empty aisle as if she'd just noticed it. "Oh!" she said. "Um, I don't know. I think Jamie's at the hunter ring, and Miguel just took Ms. Phillips's horse up there, and—"

"Whatever. I don't really care." Zara grinned. "Hey, but aren't you supposed to ride in that eq class in a few?" She stared at Kate's grungy jeans-and-T ensemble. "Because I'm not sure the judge is going to appreciate the casual look."

Kate's eyes widened, and she let out a squeak. "Oh no!" she said. "You're right, I totally lost track of the time, and I told the guys I'd tack up Fable myself—"

"Want me to help you get ready?" Zara offered. It wasn't like she had anything better to do.

"That's okay," Kate tossed over her shoulder as she rushed away. "I've got it."

"Whatever," Zara muttered, even though the other girl was already gone.

So now what? She wandered back out of the barn. Okay, so she was kind of starting to get used to her new East Coast scene. But at times like this, she was way too aware that her whole life had changed. Back in LA she never would have been hanging around by herself at a show. There were always friends around to entertain her between classes. Well, maybe "friends" was too strong a word. But people, anyway. Groupies. Suck-ups. Hangers-on. Whatever.

Not here. It was nice in a way, being anonymous. Different. But mostly kind of boring.

Deciding it was time to make her own fun, she pulled out her phone and texted Grant to say hi. He texted back within seconds:

Hey! Good to hear from u. What are u doing?

Zara glanced at the eq rings just ahead. There were some people in the warm-up by now, but still nothing happening in the ring.

So she leaned against a handy tree as she responded: *Nothing, I'm bored. Wish u were here to entertain me.*

This time his reply was even faster: *Me too! I would entertain u however u wanted!*

She grinned. Yeah, the guy was definitely hooked. She typed back quickly. *Really? Tell me what u would do.*

His response came quickly again: *First I would grab & kiss u, & then . . .*

There was more, but Zara wasn't paying attention anymore. A guy had just let himself out the rear door of one of the food kiosks nearby. Cute. Tall. Scruffy dark hair and a couple of tattoos. Maybe her age or a little older.

He glanced over and caught her looking. Zara didn't turn away, instead locking eyes with him. He looked surprised. Then his eyes slid down her body and back up, and he smiled.

Zara smiled back, wetting her lips. Yeah, suddenly she wasn't feeling so bored anymore.

Realizing her phone was still in her hand, she texted Grant back with a quick *gtg!* Then she stuck her phone in her pocket and waited for Mr. Tall, Dark, and Interesting to reach her.

Kate took a few deep breaths as she rode Fable into the ring. She hadn't stopped moving since Zara had reminded her she needed to get ready for her Big Eq class, and even so she'd barely made it to the ring on time. Her warm-up was pretty much a blur, though she did remember Jamie commenting that Fable seemed especially full of beans today.

She shot a look at Jamie now. He was leaning on the rail by the gate watching her. He gave her a thumbs-up as she rode past. "Relax," he called. "You've got this."

Kate was glad someone thought so. "Here goes nothing," she murmured as she aimed Fable at the first jump.

The early part of the course went fine. Fable was jumping well and responding instantly to her aids.

But by the time they reached the halfway point, she could feel him building speed and energy. She half-halted strongly a few times, trying to keep his impulsion in check.

"Not too fast," she murmured under her breath. "Whoa, big fella."

She squeezed the reins and held with her seat as his stride

started to open up too much. He responded a little sluggishly, almost running past the distance to a big oxer. But they pulled it off.

Three jumps left. Suddenly that seemed like way too many. Kate felt sweat beading on her face as they made the turn to the next one. Fable's ears pricked toward it, and he spurted forward again.

"No!" Kate hissed, half-halting again to get his attention back and balance him. Her arms and legs were starting to feel like rubber noodles from trying to control the strong, frisky horse.

Once again he reluctantly obeyed, rocking back on his hocks and settling into stride as they finished the approach. He sailed over easily. Two to go.

The next jump was another oxer, this one set off a long gallop halfway down the ring. Kate let Fable open up a little, figuring that might settle him.

But the plan backfired. He sped up quickly, hurtling toward the big oxer like a steeplechaser. Or at least it felt that way.

Kate half-halted frantically, willing her tired muscles to hold out just a little longer. Equitation was supposed to be all about making a tricky ride look invisible, but she stopped worrying about that, just doing whatever she could to regain control.

Fable finally responded, sort of, but it was too little too late. He met the jump on an awkward half-stride and had to twist himself sideways in the air to get over it. Luckily he was athletic enough to manage it, but Kate got jostled and the reins slipped through her hands.

As soon as he landed, Fable charged forward toward the last fence on the course. It was supposed to ride in a quiet six strides, but Kate knew there was no way that was happening. The big gray ended up doing it in five and almost chipping in again even at that. Once again he made it over, but as she pulled up, Kate knew they'd just blown any chance of pinning.

She reached forward automatically to give the horse a pat as they rode toward the gate. But inside, she was furious. Not at Fable—at herself. How could she have lost control like that?

Jamie was waiting outside the ring. "You okay?" he asked. "Looked like he got pretty strong."

"Yeah, and I couldn't do much to stop him," Kate said grimly. "Sorry, Jamie. That was totally pathetic. I don't know what happened—it was like I couldn't even half-halt well enough to get him to listen."

Jamie gave Fable a pat, then peered up at her. "Yeah, it looked like you ran out of steam toward the end of the course. That's not normal for you. I'm wondering if maybe you've been working too hard this week. Eating and sleeping too little. You do a great job taking care of things around the barn, Kate. But you've got to take care of yourself, too. I probably shouldn't have let you stick around for that colic the other night."

Kate hardly heard him. All she could focus on was the look of concern on his face. She hated disappointing Jamie. Hated it. Especially now. Here he'd offered her this amazing horse, this incredible opportunity. And what did she do? She blew it. Big-time.

But it wouldn't happen again, she vowed as Jamie turned

away to watch Summer ride in for her round. No way. She would work day and night, harder and better, whatever it took to make sure of that.

🐎

"Easy, big guy," Tommi said as Legs shifted restlessly at the end of the lead. "Come on, just one more time up and back, okay?"

The sound of the show's loudspeaker system crackled in the distance, but the shed row was deserted except for the two of them. Jamie was still out at the eq ring, Elliot had just left to take an adult client's horse to the warm-up, and the other grooms were busy elsewhere. Tommi was glad. She needed some time alone with Legs to figure out what was going on with him. She'd barely been able to stop thinking about it since leaving the warm-up ring yesterday.

Just then Legs pricked his ears and lifted his head, staring toward the end of the aisle. Turning that way, Tommi saw Kate entering, still dressed in her tidy navy show jacket and tall boots.

Tommi felt a flash of guilt. Oops. She'd meant to try to get over to the ring to watch Kate's eq trip.

"Hey," she called. "Did you already ride? How'd it go?"

Kate frowned, a dark look flashing through her eyes. "Could've been better."

Tommi knew better than to push for details. Kate would tell her about it when she was ready.

Meanwhile Kate was looking at Legs, who was pawing at the sawdust footing. "He any better today?" she asked.

"I'm not sure. Actually, do you have a sec? I could really use someone to jog him while I watch."

"Sure." Kate took the lead, giving the lanky gelding a pat. "Come on, Legs. Let's go."

She clucked and wriggled the lead, urging Legs into a trot. Tommi kept her eyes trained on the horse's legs, watching for any sign of a bobble, any shortness of stride—anything at all that wasn't what it should be. But whatever it was that she'd felt, she couldn't see it now. She sighed as Kate and Legs stopped.

"Anything?" Kate asked.

Tommi shook her head. "I'm starting to think that bitchy hotshot trainer chick was right yesterday," she muttered. "Maybe I did choke—maybe I imagined the whole thing."

"No way," Kate said. "Trust your gut. If you thought he felt off, it was better not to push him, right?"

Tommi didn't answer. Just stared at the horse, who was standing there nudging at Kate's shoulder with his muzzle, looking bored and impatient. With no clue that he held her entire future in those long, slender, oh-so-fragile legs of his.

Just then Zara wandered into view. "Hi," she said. "What are you guys doing?"

"Trying to figure out if Legs is lame or if I'm crazy," Tommi said with a loud sigh.

Zara wrinkled her nose. "You mean because of that thing yesterday? You're still obsessing over that?" She grinned. "Come on—we all know you punked out of that class because you couldn't compete with my awesome riding!"

Tommi shot her a look. "Whatever. This isn't a joke. If he's not sound enough to hold up to the show lifestyle . . ."

"Don't panic, Tommi," Kate put in softly. "It could just be an abscess or some other minor thing like that."

Zara didn't look too interested. "Hey, so did you already finish your eq class?" she asked Kate. "I meant to come over and watch, but I got, um, distracted." She smirked and licked her lips.

Even though she was still distracted by her own problems, Tommi couldn't help noticing the little gesture and wondering what it meant. Could it have something to do with Grant? He'd showed up once or twice to watch her ride at shows. Maybe he'd done the same now for Zara. It was weird to think about, and she wasn't in the mood for any more weird, so she pushed the thought away. Not her business, anyway.

"So I got there a little too late—Jamie said you'd already finished," Zara was saying. "Anyway, how'd it go?"

"It went," Kate said tightly.

"Ooookay." Zara raised an eyebrow. "Guess that means no ribbon this time, huh?"

Kate shook her head, staring at the ground. Tommi winced on her behalf. Why did she always have to be so damn hard on herself? So she'd blown a class. It happened to the best of them. Kate needed to shrug it off and move on.

"So what happened?" Zara asked. "I thought you guys were, like, the new barn superstars or whatever."

"Maybe Fable is." Kate's voice was barely audible.

Zara shrugged and returned her attention to Legs. "So what's wrong with him, anyway?" she asked, giving the gelding a pat.

"Good question," Tommi said. "I could feel he wasn't quite right when I rode him. But I can't see anything from the ground, so I'm not sure what to do about it."

"Well, that's why we have vets, I guess." Zara didn't sound too concerned. "It's not like you don't have other horses to ride."

Tommi didn't know why she'd bothered to say anything. Why she'd expected Zara to understand. How could she? She'd never taken anything seriously in her life, at least as far as Tommi could tell.

"Whatever," she said. "If he doesn't get better, my pro career could be over before it begins."

"Lighten up, *chica*," Zara said. "This is supposed to be fun, right?" She glanced from Tommi to Kate and back again. "Right?"

Kate shrugged, keeping her gaze on the floor. Tommi just rolled her eyes. In her opinion, Zara was a little *too* much about the fun. But what was the point of saying so?

The buzz of her cell phone interrupted her thoughts. It was a text from Alex:

Hi, Tommi—hope you're having a good show! Can't wait to see you when u get back on Sun. Maybe we can get together then if you're not too tired from winning all those blue ribbons & stuff?

Tommi smiled as she scanned the message. He was so sweet—and hearing from him was exactly what she needed right now. A real reminder that there was more to life than horses.

She texted him back quickly:

Sun night sounds like a plan. Will let u know tomorrow what time I'll be home, ok? ttyt!

Then Kate handed Tommi Legs's lead. "I'd better go,"

Kate said. "Javier offered to cool Fable out for me, but I know he's got other stuff to do, so . . ."

Letting her voice trail off, she rushed away down the aisle. "Wow," Zara commented. "She seems even more stressed than usual. And that's saying something."

"She's fine. Just busy, that's all." But as Tommi watched Kate disappear around the corner, she couldn't help feeling a twinge of concern. Kate *did* seem extra tense lately. Was it because Fitz wasn't at the show? Tommi wondered if maybe having him around was good for Kate after all. If there was one thing the boy knew how to do it was relax and have fun, and Kate could use a little more of that sometimes.

Then Legs shoved at her with his head, and Tommi gave him a pat.

"Okay, mister," she told him. "We're not accomplishing anything here. Let's get you back to your stall."

EIGHT

— — — — —

"Whoa!" Zara stopped short in the doorway, staring into the loft.

The place was a wreck. Empty bottles and cans lying around everywhere. Overturned furniture. The TV playing static.

"Hello?" she called, stepping over a stray sofa cushion as she walked in. "Stacie?"

No answer. Zara dropped her suitcase and boots near the door. The apartment smelled as bad as it looked. Stacie must've partied all weekend and then some.

Just then she heard the clatter of footsteps at the top of the stairwell behind her. "Hi!" Stacie exclaimed breathlessly. "Didn't you hear me calling you? I was just coming around the corner when I saw you getting out of your friend's car. Nice wheels, by the way."

"That's Tommi," Zara said. "Her dad's like the richest guy on the planet or something." She glanced at the brown paper bag in her cousin's hand. "Where were you? Out buying a mop?"

"Huh? No, I just ran over to that organic market around the corner." Stacie held up the bag and shook it, grinning. "Scored these awesome local peaches. What does that say to you?"

Zara just stared at her. "What?"

"It's daiquiri time!" Stacie sang out. "How about that? Does your babysitter take care of you, or what?"

Zara hesitated, taking another look around at the mess. Then she shrugged. She'd had a great show—why not celebrate?

"Bring it on," she said. "I love daiquiris."

Tommi was in her room, staring into her closet, when there was a knock at her door. "Come in," she called, distracted.

She was supposed to meet Alex in half an hour, and she was running late. Traffic on the New Jersey Turnpike had been even worse than usual coming back from the show. Plus she'd had to come in through the Holland Tunnel to drop Zara in SoHo, which had added even more time to the trip.

The door opened, and her father stuck his head in. He was wearing his rimless reading glasses and holding the *Times* business section.

"Thought I heard you come in," he said. "Have a good show? How'd our boy do?"

Tommi hesitated. So far she'd kept things pretty vague whenever her father asked how Legs was coming along. That seemed to be enough for him. He didn't really want to know every detail of the horse's training. All he cared about was results.

But this time she couldn't just say "Fine" and leave it at that. Not without actually lying to him. That didn't mean she was going to mention that her trip to the Hamptons had meant Legs had stood in a show stall for several days without much work, or that she still wondered if that was why he hadn't seemed quite right when she'd finally gotten on him. No, there was no way she was going to tell her father *that*.

"I had to scratch him this time," she said. "He felt a little funny in the warm-up on Friday."

Looking concerned, her father stepped into the room. "What's wrong with him? Is it serious?"

"Probably not."

"Probably?" Tommi's father frowned. "What, didn't you have a vet look at him?"

"Not yet." Tommi grabbed a Rag & Bone sheer blouse out of her closet and tossed it on her bed. She looked great in it, and Alex hadn't seen it yet. "I'll have Jamie's vet take a look this week if necessary," she told her father. "But he was already feeling better when I took him for a hack around the grounds this morning."

Her father was still frowning. "I don't understand. Is there something wrong with this horse or not?"

Tommi shrugged. "Nothing I could quite put my finger on," she said. "Jamie couldn't see anything. Legs just didn't feel right. Call it a gut feeling, I guess."

"A gut feeling?" Now Tommi's father was starting to look annoyed. "Listen, Thomasina, this isn't a game of My Little Pony. You're playing with real money here."

"I know that," Tommi said quickly, trying to head off one of his patented financial-responsibility lectures.

Too late. "It's one thing to protect the health of this horse if there's really something wrong. That's just common sense and good business. But a gut feeling? Really? You have a responsibility to your investors—that's you and me, in case you've forgotten—to maximize returns. You need to push forward and sell this animal, not get all namby-pamby overcautious about every little step he takes."

Tommi was starting to feel annoyed herself. What did her father know about horses, anyway? That would be pretty much a big fat zippo. Last she'd noticed, he couldn't even tell her junior hunter from her eq horse, even though they were totally different heights, body types, and shades of bay.

"Whatever," she said. "I hear you, Oh Great Financial Wizard, okay? I'm dealing with it."

Grabbing the blouse off her bed and her favorite pair of jeans from the pile of clean laundry Mrs. Grigoryan had left on a chair, she stomped into her bathroom and slammed the door behind her. She really didn't want to think about investments or maximizing profits or anything like that right now. All she wanted to do was get dressed for her date with Alex so she could go out and have a good time and not worry about any of this for a while.

Kate could hear shouting even before she opened the front door. All her father, of course. Her mother never raised her voice.

She hesitated, tempted to back away and take off again. But where would she go? It was well after 10:00 p.m. Jamie had shooed her home from the barn after she'd spent the past couple of hours helping the grooms clean out the trailers and settle the horses in. The usual Sunday-night postshow routine. Now all she wanted was food, shower, and sleep. In that order.

Taking a deep breath, she went in. Her parents were both in the front room. The TV was tuned to some cooking show, volume muted. Her mother was sitting on the worn plaid couch with four candlesticks, a rag, and a tub of brass cleaner set out on the coffee table in front of her. Kate's father, still in his cop's uniform, was pacing back and forth between his wife and the TV.

". . . and if we don't beat some sense into that boy now, it'll be too late!" he was yelling when Kate came in. "He has to know there are consequences to the dumb-ass things he's doing!"

"Please don't shout, William," her mother said in her soft, feeble voice. "Andy already explained that he had no idea the police would have any reason to break up that party. He just went along with his friends, that's all."

Kate winced. Great. So her younger brother was up to more trouble. Ever since he'd turned fourteen and started hanging out with a new bunch of friends, it had been all downhill with him. He'd skipped so much school last year that he had to go to summer school. That wasn't going too well, either, since he'd ditched his very first day and probably 50 percent of those since. Now it sounded like he was in even more trouble.

Her father heard the door shut behind her. "Katie!" he said, his voice softening. "You're home."

"I'm home," Kate said lightly. Pretending she hadn't just heard them fighting. That she didn't know what was going on.

"Good." Her mother stood up. "Now that you're home safely, I'm going to bed. Good night."

Not meeting either her husband or daughter's eye, she rushed out of the room. Kate's father watched her go with a heavy sigh, then turned to Kate again.

"You hungry? Come on, I'll make you a sandwich."

He headed toward the kitchen without waiting for a response. Kate dropped her stuff at the foot of the stairs, then followed. She slid onto one of the stools at the butcher-block island, watching her father dig into the refrigerator.

"Ham and Swiss okay?" he asked.

"Yeah, fine," Kate said.

He tossed a loaf of bread on the island, along with a couple of deli packages and a tub of mayo. "So how was the show?" he asked, turning away to grab a plate out of a cabinet.

"Good," Kate said. "I did the eq again on that fancy horse Jamie's been letting me ride. Didn't pin, though."

"Hmm." Her father's big, callused hands were already busy putting together her sandwich. He didn't know much about horses or showing—thanks to his work schedule, he rarely got to come watch her ride anymore. But usually he at least pretended to be interested in the details. Tonight, she could tell he was too distracted to care.

"You probably heard your mother and me arguing when you came in, Katie," he said, turning away to grab the mustard out of the fridge. "I don't want you to worry. It's just your brother—growing pains, I guess you could call it. It's upsetting your mother quite a bit, and well . . ."

He let his voice trail off. Kate just sat there, wishing she could be anywhere else. Cleaning a stall. Stacking itchy hay bales. Anything.

Her father finally turned back and met her eye. "Nobody ever said life was always a field full of daffodils," he said with a sigh. "Seems like maybe this is one of those no-daffodils times for this family." He reached over and touched her on the arm. "I'm just glad you're still your same good, normal self, Katie. Makes things a little easier knowing that, anyway."

Kate forced a smile, not knowing what to say. Her father squirted some mustard on the sandwich, slapped on the top piece of bread, and set it in front of her.

"There you go," he said. "Eat up, then get some sleep." He shot a look toward the master bedroom across the narrow back hallway. "I'm going to try to talk to your mother."

As soon as he left, Kate felt herself start to shake. Her father seemed to think she had it all figured out. That she was just as happy and single-minded as she'd been as a little girl, back when the only thing she had to worry about was earning enough money pulling weeds or walking dogs to pay for her next ride at Happy Acres.

Little did he know how hard she was working right now

just to hold it together. Or how quickly everything seemed to be spinning out of control. That disaster with Ford, and the way the secret kept gnawing at her. The way she'd let Jamie and Fable down in her eq class. Even her relationship with Fitz felt too shaky for comfort—sure, things were good again now, but for how long? How could it possibly last when they were so different?

She felt sick to her stomach at the thought of it all. Although she suddenly realized that feeling might also have something to do with being hungry—she hadn't eaten since splitting a bad horse-show burger with Dani at lunch, many hours earlier. The scents of ham, mustard, and mayo wafted up, making her forget everything else for a moment.

Grabbing the sandwich, she opened her mouth to shove it in, ready to wolf down the whole thing in one bite. But she stopped herself before she actually did it. Things were bad enough right now without pigging out and making herself *really* sick. She couldn't afford to wake up with a stomachache because she'd eaten too much too late at night. At least she should be able to manage to avoid that, even if she couldn't seem to handle a fresh horse anymore, or a fresh guy.

Kate set the sandwich back on the plate, then grabbed the knife her father had dropped on the counter. Carefully pressing the dull blade into the soft bread, she cut the sandwich into four equal sections. Then she picked up one of the sections and ate it, taking small bites and chewing carefully to make it last. She'd read in some magazine somewhere that it was healthier to eat that way, anyhow.

When she finished, she stared at the other three sections

for a second. She thought about eating one more. But no—
she'd already decided that one was safer. If she didn't have
the strength to stick to a stupid decision like that, how could
she ever expect to get the rest of her life in order?

Grabbing the plate, she quickly dumped the rest of the
sandwich in the trash before she could weaken. Good. That
was done. She felt better immediately, stronger, even though
her stomach was still grumbling a little.

But that was okay. She could handle that. No problem.

NINE

— — — — —

Zara woke up, rolled over to look at the clock on her bedside table, and groaned. Almost two in the afternoon.

"Ugh," she muttered, her mouth feeling cottony and gross. She was pretty sure it was Tuesday, which meant she was supposed to be at Pelham Lane for the juniors' group lesson in a couple of hours. What time had she finally passed out last night, anyway? She couldn't remember. Stacie had invited some people over—again—and things had ended up getting pretty crazy.

Zara rolled over and lurched to her feet. Stumbling over to her bathroom, she stuck her head under the cold-water tap until she started to feel more human.

Soon she was out on the landing overlooking the main room. The place was a wreck, but that was no surprise. Stacie hadn't bothered to clean up at all after the last few parties. Why should this one be any different?

The surprise was that this time, not all the partyers had

gone home. And not just whichever lucky guy Stacie chose to let pass out on top of her, either. This time there were three or four strangers sleeping it off down there, nestled into various sofas and chairs and, in one case, sprawled on the floor under a table.

"Great," Zara said aloud. "Fabulous. Just what I need."

She stomped down to the guest room at the other end of the row of bedrooms. When Zara glanced in through the half-open door, some short, stocky guy with a hairy back was flat out and snoring on the big double bed. No Stacie. Zara even tiptoed in to check the bathroom, but her cousin wasn't in there, either.

Okay, now what? Zara was heading for the stairs when she heard her phone ringing in her room. She dashed in and grabbed it off her bedside table. To her surprise, the caller ID read: GINA GIRARD.

"Mom?" Zara blurted out, pressing the phone to her ear. "Is that really you?"

"Zara, my love!" Her mother's warm, melodious voice poured into her ear. "How are you? I miss you like crazy!"

"Me too." Zara sank down onto the edge of her bed. "Where are you calling from?"

"The set here in Vancouver." Gina sighed. "There's some kind of trouble with some permit or something, and it's causing all sorts of delays. Since I'm just standing around twiddling my thumbs here, I decided it was the perfect time to call and check in on how my favorite daughter's doing."

She was Gina's *only* daughter, but Zara smiled anyway. She hadn't spoken to her mother in almost two weeks, and until now hadn't realized how much she'd actually missed her.

"Everything's cool," she said. "I'm totally showing New York who's boss."

Gina laughed. "I bet you are," she said. "But listen, your dad told me about your cousin coming to stay. How's that going? You two girls getting along all right?"

Zara hesitated, her gaze straying through the open doorway to the overlook. Living in a nonstop party zone was getting a little old, and there was a really easy way to put a stop to it. All she had to do was tell her mother the truth about everything that had been going on, and Stacie would be on a bus back to Southeast BumbleFlip as fast as she could pack up her mall-slut wardrobe.

"Um, it's fine," she said. "I mean, I told Zac I didn't need a babysitter, but whatever."

Sure, Stacie was getting a little carried away with the partying. So what? Zara wasn't going to narc her out. She wasn't like that.

"I know you think you're grown up enough to stay alone, love," her mom said. "But your dad and I both feel better knowing someone's there with you."

Yeah. Zara glanced out toward the main room again. What would Gina say if she could see just how many people were keeping her company in the loft right now?

"So how's the movie going?" she asked, deciding it was time for a change of subject. "Have to kiss any fat old has-beens with bad breath?"

Like any actor Zara had ever met, her mother didn't need a second invitation to talk about herself. She launched into a vivid description of every step of the movie-making process as if revealing the meaning of life.

Finally Zara cut her off in the middle of some boring story about one of the makeup artists. "Listen, Mom, I've got to go," she said. "I have a riding lesson today."

"Sounds fun," Gina said. "I should go, too. There's a reporter visiting the set today from one of the big news weeklies, and I don't want to let my costars hog all the free publicity!" Her musical laugh sounded tinny over the phone. "Talk to you soon, my love!"

"Bye, Mom." Zara hung up and walked over to her closet to see if she had any clean breeches. She was going to have to book if she didn't want to be late. Jamie really hated it when anyone was late.

But wait. How the hell was she supposed to get to the barn? Stacie was supposed to be playing chauffeur as part of her Zara-sitting duties. But even if she happened to turn up in the next few minutes, Zara somehow doubted her cousin was in any condition for the hour-plus drive up to Westchester County. At least based on her condition the last time she recalled seeing her, somewhere around 3:00 a.m.

"Shit," she said. For a second she thought about calling Tommi. Okay, so she probably wouldn't be thrilled to drive all the way downtown to pick her up, especially after last time. But maybe Zara could hop the subway up to Tommi's place. She just needed to take the E train to the 4-5-6. Or was it the 1 to the 7? Dammit, she still couldn't keep all the different lines and transfers straight. Back in LA, nobody ever even thought about taking the pathetic excuse for a subway, so who could blame her for having trouble?

Anyway, she realized it was way too late for any of that. Tommi was probably at the barn already, or at least on her way.

"Car service it is, then," Zara said aloud with a shrug. Zac would just have to deal with the bill. And if he had a problem with it, he could take it up with Nanny Stacie.

Zara showered and dressed as fast as she could, then headed downstairs, hoping some drunken loser hadn't puked on her boots wherever she'd left them. One of the crashers was upright by now. He was sitting on the leather sofa, staring around with bleary eyes, as if wondering where he'd woken up this time.

"I don't suppose you made breakfast, did you?" Zara asked as she passed him.

"Huh?" The guy blinked at her, his mouth falling open.

"Never mind." Zara spotted her boots wedged under a table. Grabbing them and stuffing them into her bag, she headed for the door.

Just before she reached it, it swung open. "Oh, you're up!" Stacie exclaimed, hurrying in. "I got bagels." She held up a bulging white paper bag.

"No time," Zara snapped, pushing past her. "I'm late. Oh, and by the way, thanks for the ride."

Stacie looked confused. "Huh? Zara, wait—"

But Zara wasn't in the mood. She kept moving, bypassing the elevator and heading straight down the stairs without looking back.

Kate dashed into the tack room to hang up the half dozen bridles she'd just finished cleaning. She was moving so fast she almost crashed into someone.

"Sorry!" she said, skidding to a stop just in time. Then she saw it was Joy, Jamie's assistant trainer. "Oh! It's you."

"None other." Joy was carrying a saddle with a girth slung over it. "Just heading out to the big jumping ring to school that new horse before you guys head in there for your lesson."

"Listen, I've been meaning to thank you," Kate told Joy. "I really, really, totally appreciate you agreeing to cover for me on Saturday so I can go to my friend's horse show." She stepped over and started hanging up the bridles. Her hands flew as she expertly threaded each one into a tidy figure-eight on its assigned hook.

"And I told you, it's no big deal." Joy smiled. "We should be able to survive without you for one day. Barely."

Kate smiled back sheepishly. "I know. But Saturdays are always crazy when it's a nonshowing weekend, and there are those two new pony kids starting that I was supposed to show around—"

"Kate, seriously. Chill." Joy shifted the saddle to her other arm as the girth began to slip off. "We'll be fine. And you deserve a Saturday off once in a while."

Kate just nodded, trying to remember the last Saturday she'd spent anywhere but at Pelham Lane or a show. But that sort of mental exercise was a waste of time, so she banished it quickly.

"Okay," she said. "I just wanted you to know I appreciate it."

"Message received." Joy saluted with her free hand and hurried out of the room.

Kate finished hanging up the bridles, then checked her watch. Still almost an hour before she had to start tacking up for the group lesson. She was debating whether to use the time to pick up manure in the paddocks or clip a couple of ponies when Fitz sauntered in.

"Hi, gorgeous," he said. "I was hoping I might find you here."

He looked tall and relaxed and handsome as always, his reddish-blond hair windblown from driving too fast in his convertible, his Psycho Bunny polo hanging just right on his lean but broad-shouldered frame. Nice, though Kate was much more interested in how his whole face had lit up as soon as he'd seen her, which made her feel happy and breathless and maybe a little confused all at once. But mostly good. Being at the show all week without him, it had been way too easy to second-guess their relationship. To remember the bad moments and downplay the good stuff. But now? Seeing the way Fitz was smiling at her made her wonder exactly what she'd been so worried about.

"Hi!" she said as he leaned in for a kiss. "What are you doing here so early?"

"I couldn't wait a second longer to see you." Fitz rested one hand on the small of her back, using the other to gently push aside a few strands of blond hair that had come loose from Kate's ponytail. "I wanted to come by on Sunday night to welcome you home from the show, but my parents had me chained in the dungeon. And I tried to come out yesterday, but Jamie had a pack of wild dogs tied to the gate to keep me out."

Kate grimaced, knowing he was probably only exaggerating a little. His parents couldn't be thrilled that they'd been forced to shell out somewhere in the high five figures for a lame horse. As for Jamie, well, the barn was supposed to be closed to clients on Mondays. It was the day when Kate and the other workers got a chance to catch up on things that didn't get done the rest of the week. Normally Jamie didn't mind if a boarder wanted to sneak in a quick hack, especially the more serious competitors, as long as they tacked up and cooled out their own horses. Somehow, though, Kate doubted he would welcome any extra sightings of Fitz right now.

But she didn't worry about any of that for long as Fitz cupped the back of her head with his hand, pulling her face toward his. Their lips met, and for a while Kate didn't think about anything but kissing him.

Finally they came up for air. "Wow," Fitz said. "That was almost worth waiting a whole week for."

Kate smiled. "Yeah."

"Listen, there's still plenty of time before our lesson, and I'm only getting bread and water at home." Fitz checked his Breitling watch. "I grabbed some falafel on my way out of town, and I've got enough to share. How about we sneak away for a little picnic, just the two of us? It'll be like a mini-date."

"A picnic?" Kate hesitated. On the one hand, she was supposed to be working today. But she felt as if she'd barely spent any time with Fitz lately.

He put both arms around her again, pulling her closer. "Come on," he whispered in her ear, his breath tickling her skin. "Say yes. I needs me some quality Kate time."

She shivered, pressing up against him. "Well," she said slowly, trying to calculate how late she'd have to stay tonight to make up for taking a little time off now. "I guess I do have to eat. But I can't stay long."

A few minutes later the two of them were on the little hill

behind the barn overlooking the back pasture, where a couple of retired horses grazed contentedly in the shade of several old sycamores. Fitz had borrowed one of his horses' fancy monogrammed wool show coolers, which he'd spread on the grass as a makeshift picnic blanket. He'd grabbed sodas from the fridge in the office, a roll of paper towels from the supply room, and even a blossom off the climbing rose that rambled over the post-and-rail fence by the parking lot.

Kate watched as he dumped several Styrofoam containers of food out of a couple of greasy paper bags, then set the rose on top of one of them with a flourish. "Lunch is served," he announced. "Dig in."

"Thanks." Kate didn't have the heart to tell him that she didn't much care for falafel, or most other Middle Eastern food for that matter. Spotting a chunk of grilled chicken in one of the containers, she carefully picked it out.

Fitz popped some falafel into his mouth. "So here's some good news," he said. "My house arrest is finally over. The 'rents said I can go to the next show. I think it's just 'cause they're tired of looking at me, but hey, I'll take it."

"That's great!" Kate felt as if she should say something more. Something about how it wasn't fair, that he shouldn't have taken the fall for Zara's mistake in the first place. Something to show how much she appreciated what he'd done for her. But she couldn't come up with the right words, so instead just added, "Um, we missed you at the last one."

"We?" Fitz paused in the middle of scooping up some hummus with a scrap of pita and cocked one eyebrow. "Who exactly do you mean by *we*?"

"You know. All of us." Kate felt herself blushing. "Come on, you know what I mean."

He grinned. "I'm a little slow. You'd better explain it to me."

"Stop it. I missed you, okay? Although I'm kind of starting to wonder why." She rolled her eyes in mock exasperation.

"That's more like it. And you already know I missed you, too. Like crazy." He blew her a kiss, then turned his attention back to his food. "So what else did I miss last week, anyway? Who did what, who won what, what's all the gossip?"

After that the two of them fell into an easy, comfortable conversation about the last show, the next show, and various other topics. Finally Fitz pushed the food away and let out a burp.

"Sorry," he said with a grin. "In some cultures that's a sign of respect for the food. Or for the chef. Something like that."

Kate smiled, glad that he didn't seem to notice that she hadn't really eaten much other than a roll and a few more scraps of chicken. This picnic had been such a sweet gesture; she didn't want to ruin it. "You've got hummus on your chin," she said. "Is that a sign of respect, too?"

"Totally." Fitz grabbed a paper towel and took a swipe at his face. "Did I get it?"

"No." Kate leaned across the jumble of food boxes and plucked the paper towel out of his hand. "Here, let me."

She dabbed at the spot of hummus. Fitz grabbed her wrist and pulled her closer. "I think I see some hummus on your lips," he said, his voice suddenly going softer. "Let me get that for you."

Kate didn't bother to point out that she hadn't eaten any

hummus. "Careful," she said instead. "Jamie might not like it if I show up for our lesson with falafel ground into the knees of my breeches."

In response, Fitz used his free hand to sweep the food containers, used napkins, and empty soda cans aside. "Better?" he asked.

Without waiting for an answer, he scooted closer, dropping her wrist and wrapping his arms around her. Kate tried not to think about how much time had passed, how much she still wanted to get done before it was time to tack up for the lesson.

Then his lips met hers, and she stopped thinking about any of that.

TEN

▬▬ ▬▬ ▬▬ ▬▬ ▬▬

"Trot," Tommi said with a cluck, jiggling the long whip she was holding in her right hand. Her other hand was on the lunge line attached to Legs's halter. She was out in the deserted flat-work ring, lungeing him to see how he was moving.

The horse curled his neck and snorted as he jumped into an extended trot. After only a few strides, he broke into a brisk canter, kicking up his heels as he spun around her in a circle at the end of the line.

Tommi smiled, glad that he seemed to be feeling good. But she didn't want him to get too excited and hurt himself.

"Eeeeeasy," she said. "Trot."

Using her voice and body language, she managed to bring him back to the slower gait. This time he settled into a long, low hunter frame and trotted nicely. His legs moved evenly, like clockwork, and even though Tommi never took her eyes off the horse, she couldn't see even the slightest bobble, hitch, or hesitation in his stride.

"Okay, walk on," she called to the horse, once again positioning her body to slow him down.

He slowed to a walk, and she reeled him in and gave him a pat. She'd given him a couple of days off after returning from the show. He'd had his usual turnout, but she hadn't ridden or worked with him at all. Now he seemed to be back to normal. Maybe the rest and turnout had been all he'd needed to recover from whatever had been bothering him that day.

If so, what did that mean for his future? Was it a fluke, just one of those passing things that could bother any athlete now and then? Or could it be a harbinger of more trouble to come? A show horse lived much of his life on the road, standing on trailers and in small stalls, sometimes working on less-than-ideal footing. What if Legs couldn't handle all that, either physically or mentally? Some horses couldn't.

And what about her? Was she really cut out for the tough life of a horse professional? Looking back over the past week and a half, she had to admit she hadn't made a very good start of it. One tempting invitation from a cute guy, and she'd blown off her plans and run away to the Hamptons as if she didn't have a care in the world.

She couldn't quite regret that decision. Not when it had meant getting to know Alex so much better. But now there was this thing with Legs, and she was feeling anxious and uncertain about what it meant. She hated feeling that way—she hated it a lot.

"Come on, boy." She unhooked the lunge line as she prepared to take Legs back to his stall. "I've got to go get Toccata ready for my lesson."

A little while later she rode into the jumping ring. Jamie hadn't arrived yet, but a few of the other juniors were there warming up their horses.

Summer was trotting past the gate when Tommi came in, but she brought her horse to a walk and stared at her. "Hey, you're riding Toccata today," she said. "Does that mean Legs is still lame?"

"He's not lame," Tommi snapped. "He was never lame."

Summer raised her eyebrows. "Oooookay," she said. "I guess I must have imagined watching you scratch from that jumper class last weekend. Anyway, I was just going to say it's nice to see you on Toccata. You two are always amazing together."

"Thanks," Tommi said, not sure whether to feel more annoyed by Summer's typical sucking up or guilty for snapping at the girl for a relatively innocent comment. "I just meant Legs wasn't really *lame* lame. I just wasn't sure he—whatever. It doesn't matter."

Suddenly sick of thinking about it, she picked up her reins and sent Toccata into a trot. All she wanted to do for the next hour was turn off her brain and ride.

Halfway to the tack room, Kate could already hear the others laughing and talking. The scents of hot tomato sauce, cheese, and garlic drifting down the aisle were as familiar as those of hay and horses. Time for the juniors' postlesson pizza.

Fitz waved when she came in. He was lounging against an empty saddle rack shoving pizza into his mouth. She felt herself blush as her mind jumped back to their private little picnic earlier—especially the last part, after Fitz had finished eating. They'd lost track of time and almost been late to the lesson, but Kate couldn't quite manage to be sorry about that. Still, she did her best to push aside the memories, not wanting anyone else to guess what she was thinking.

Everyone else was already there. Tommi, Marissa, and Zara were sitting on the bench. Summer was standing nearby, waving her hands around as she talked to them. Dani had just grabbed another slice, stepping over Jamie's bulldog to get it. As usual, Chaucer was planted right in front of the boxes on the bandage trunk, while the younger dogs worked the room, begging for scraps.

"Hi," Kate said to Fitz, bending over to grab a slice of plain cheese from one of the boxes. "What's all the excitement?"

Fitz smirked. "Summer's just whining because she got shut out in the eq. Again."

Summer heard him and looked over. "Shut up," she said. "You know I'm totally right. That girl only pinned higher than me because her mother's head trainer at that big barn on Long Island, and the judge obviously knew it."

"Get over it, Summer," Dani said. "That girl beat you because she's ridden like ten horses a day since she was in diapers."

Marissa picked a gob of gooey cheese off her pizza and fed it to one of the dogs. "Yeah. Or if anything gives her an edge, it's that she's even taller and skinnier than Kate." She glanced down at herself with a rueful smile. "Which pretty much explains why I never pin in the eq."

Dani, Tommi, and Fitz laughed, but Summer shot Kate an irritated glance. "Being tall and skinny didn't help Kate much this time, did it?" she snapped. "Even *I* beat her. And I'm not tall, or a trainer's kid, or even a working student who gets fancy horses to ride for free anytime she wants. So there!" She flounced over and grabbed another slice of pepperoni.

Kate froze in mid-bite, suddenly feeling like some kind of gangly eight-foot-tall beanpole freak. Was that really what Summer and the others thought of her? That she only won because Jamie gave her horses to ride for free? What did any of these people know about her, anyway? What did they know about all the work she had to put in to earn those rides?

Tommi frowned. "Shut the hell up, Summer," she said. "Don't take it out on Kate just because you're feeling pissy about your own riding."

"Yeah." Marissa giggled. "Look on the bright side—at least you didn't do a face plant over the first jump like that poor kid from Maple Mount whose horse tripped . . ."

Kate didn't hear the rest. Fitz had just stepped around the trunk and sidled up next to her. She was so distracted she almost choked on the big bite of pizza in her mouth. Swallowing it down in a loud gulp, she smiled up at him uncertainly.

"Don't pay any attention to Summer, gorgeous," he whispered, slipping an arm around her shoulders. "She's just jealous because you're hotter *and* more talented than she is."

Kate just shrugged, shooting the other girls a glance. She still felt self-conscious, as if everyone in the room was judging everything about her, even though the others had already moved on to gossiping about someone else. She set down her pizza, suddenly not in the mood for this.

"I should go help the guys turn out horses," she said.

"I've got a better idea. Let's go for a walk—just the two of us." Fitz gave her arm a squeeze. "What do you say?"

Kate hesitated, glancing up into his playful hazel eyes. Seeing the way he was looking at her made her shiver without really knowing why. She flashed back to their picnic again—and then to that night in the hay stall. He'd been so sweet since then, so eager to make it up to her. Was he for real?

Whatever. Tommi and the others might think she was naive, but Kate couldn't help believing—or was it hoping?—that Fitz was sincere. That he actually thought she was something special.

"Okay, I guess," she said. "But I can't hang out for long. I mean it this time."

He smiled, grabbed her hand, and pulled her out of the room. Kate was pretty sure she saw Tommi glance at them as they left, but the others didn't seem to notice their departure. Good.

Fitz led her down the aisle and around the corner into the feed room. Then he dropped her hand, took her by the shoulders, and gently turned her to face him.

"This is more like it," he said. "Come here."

He pulled her in for a kiss. Kate sank into him, feeling the tension seep out of her body again. For a second she forgot about everything else as their mouths explored each other.

Then she felt his hands start to wander. "Hey," she said softly, pulling away and pushing his hands back where they belonged.

"Sorry," he said in a low, husky voice, a sheepish smile playing on his lips as he pulled her close again. "Force of habit. I'll be good—I swear."

To her surprise, he was. At least mostly. A couple of times things started to get more intense, but he always pulled back before it got uncomfortable. For a while Kate drifted along in a pleasant haze, letting what was happening between them happen; not thinking, just feeling.

Then some small part of her mind started to wonder: How long was he going to be happy with things the way they were? He'd put it all on the line for her, risked his parents' wrath and Jamie's, just to show he was sorry for pushing too hard that night. Didn't she owe him more than this? Wasn't he going to expect more sooner or later, or could he possibly mean it when he said he'd do anything to be with her?

She started to get that sour feeling in the pit of her stomach again. The same one she'd had the other night while talking to her dad after the big blowup. The same one that had attacked her at the show when she'd seen Jamie waiting at the gate for her after that eq round. Why did they all keep trying so hard, believing she could be what they wanted her to be, when she couldn't seem to live up to any of it?

Her body tensed. Fitz felt it and pulled back. He put one finger under her chin, tilting her face up so he could look into her eyes.

"What?" he whispered. "You seem kind of—I don't know, like you're spacing out all of a sudden. You getting tired of me already?"

His words were light, but she saw real doubt in his eyes. She shook her head.

"Sorry," she said. "It's not you at all. Guess I'm just distracted."

"By what?"

She shrugged, not sure what to say.

"Come on, Kate." He caressed her cheekbone lightly with one finger. "You can trust me."

She hesitated. Could she? She felt really close to him right now—as close as she'd felt to anyone in a long time. But how could someone like him ever understand what she was going through? Fitz sailed through life like he owned the world. Which his family pretty much did, come to think of it. He couldn't know what it was like to be her, to have her family, her problems. Her life.

He was still staring at her. Waiting. She had to tell him something.

"It's just—uh, my friend Natalie," she blurted out without really thinking, just latching on to the first thing she could think of that didn't directly involve him or the barn. "Um, we've been, you know, kind of drifting apart lately, and now she invited me out to her barn on Saturday."

"Wait. You mean that lesson barn where you first learned to ride?" he asked. "Happy something, right?"

She nodded, a little surprised that he remembered. "Yeah. Happy Acres. They're having a show, and Nat's all excited about some new project horse she's working with, and, well, I guess I'm just a little nervous about going back there."

Fitz smiled, his finger tracing the outline of her chin. "Dr. Hall's got the perfect solution to your problem," he said. "I'll come with. You know, like for moral support."

"What?" Kate blurted out in surprise. "Wait, you don't have to do that. It's just a dinky little beginner-type schooling show, and I'm sure you have better stuff to do on Saturday."

"Nothing better than spending the day with my favorite girl." Fitz shrugged. "Besides, it'll be fun. Jamie's always telling us to observe other riders and stuff, right?"

Kate wasn't sure the Happy Acres show was quite what Jamie had in mind. Still, what could she say?

"Um, okay, if you're sure—" she began.

"Sure I'm sure." Fitz grinned down at her. "It's a date."

Kate smiled back weakly, trying not to imagine what Nat was going to say when she showed up with Fitz. Talk about worlds colliding . . .

ELEVEN

At 10:30 a.m. on a Friday, the Upper East Side bistro was sleepy and quiet. That suited Tommi just fine. She and Alex had the place to themselves except for a trio of old ladies gossiping over tea and a harried-looking young nanny with a couple of little kids in strollers.

"I'm glad this worked out," Tommi said, reaching for the salt.

Alex looked extra adorable that day in a button-down shirt and loosely knotted funky vintage tie. "Me too," he said. "It almost makes coming into the city to see my great-aunt Koo-Koo—I mean Kiku—bearable." He raised one eyebrow. "Sure you don't want to come along and meet her?"

"Tempting. But can't." Tommi shrugged. "Like I said, I'm heading out to the barn after this."

"Bummer for me. You have a riding lesson or something?" He grinned. "By the way, how come you still have to take so many lessons? I thought you already knew how to ride."

She rolled her eyes. "Yeah, I never heard *that* one before."

They both laughed. Tommi was finding that she laughed a lot when she was with Alex. She liked that.

"Anyway, for your information, there's no lesson today," she said. "Our group lesson is almost always on Tuesday, and I'll probably do a private with Joy tomorrow."

"Cool. So on Tuesdays you ride with all the other people your age, right? Like Zac Trask's daughter and all of them?"

"Yeah. There are about seven of us who usually ride together." Tommi took a sip of her iced tea. "It's fun to hear their feedback and watch how other people handle stuff. Like, this week we worked on this cool exercise where we had to take three jumps on a serpentine, and one of the girls—Marissa—was having trouble with her horse bulging out on the turns, and she got a little rattled."

She glanced over at Alex, expecting him to look bored. But he'd actually put down his fork to listen. "I get it," he said. "So you can watch the others ride and figure out how to deal yourself when it's your turn. So how'd your horse do? Were you riding that one you're trying to sell? You said he can be hard to steer when he's excited."

Tommi was impressed. So he *had* been listening to her all this time—not just faking interest to win her over.

"Actually, I didn't ride Legs this time. I still wasn't sure he was totally back to normal and didn't want to take any chances, so I rode Toccata. He's my junior hunter—he's awesome." She smiled, remembering how it had felt to just relax and let her horse do his job. "I'm kind of glad I rode him in the lesson. I'd almost forgotten how fun and easy it can be, you know? Just riding, doing your thing, without worrying about whether you're screwing up his training, or how you're ever going to sell him when you can't even get him to pick up his right lead or whatever."

Alex nodded. "Makes sense," he said. "It's like me just jamming with my friends in somebody's spare room versus trying to put together an actual demo tape or something."

"Exactly. Not that I'm not complaining," Tommi added quickly. "Legs is great. It's just sometimes nice to remind myself why I want to do this in the first place."

"I hear you." Alex smiled at the waitress who'd just appeared to refill their water glasses. "So is that why you're going to the barn today? To ride Legs?"

"I might hop on if there's time," Tommi said. "But he's felt good all week, so I might just give him today off. I'm mostly going out to meet my friend Kate so we can hit the tack store near the barn."

"Tack store?"

"That's where you buy horse stuff," Tommi explained. "I need to pick up a new pair of bell boots for Legs. Plus I'm getting bored with all my show shirts—might just have to pick up a few new ones for the next show."

Alex laughed. "Okay, I was just going to try to invite myself along," he joked. "But some girly shopping trip where you'll be trying on clothes and crap like that? Sorry, not even for you. Still, it sounds like you guys have lots of fun at the barn. I'd love to check it out sometime. Maybe you could teach me to ride."

"Really? Sure, that'd be fun. Just let me know when you

want to do it." Tommi smiled, then checked her watch. "Uh-oh, I'd better hurry. I don't want to be late to meet Kate." She grabbed her sandwich and took another bite.

"What's the big deal?" Alex said. "Just tell her traffic was bad on the bridge."

"That's not the point. Today's her day off, and she'll probably have to disguise herself to sneak into the barn and meet me." Seeing his look of confusion, she added, "Kate's a working student—she works for Jamie in exchange for rides and stuff. Her family doesn't have a ton of money, so that's the only way she can afford to ride there."

"So?" Alex waved at the waitress to get her attention. "What's the big deal about showing up at the barn on her day off? I'd think your trainer would be glad for a little free help."

"Yeah, normally he probably would. But Kate's different." Tommi thought about how to explain Kate to someone who didn't know her. "She'd probably work twenty-four/seven if Jamie let her. Like, literally almost. He pretty much had to banish her from even coming to the barn on her day off to keep her from burning herself out."

Soon they were stepping out onto the sunbaked sidewalk in front of the restaurant. Alex immediately pulled out a pair of sunglasses and put them on. Paired with his shirt and tie, faded jeans, and spiky dark hair, they made him look cuter than ever. Acting on impulse, Tommi slipped an arm around his waist.

"Walk me to my car?" she said.

He put his arm around her shoulders and squeezed. "Absolutely," he said. "Anything to put off visiting you-know-who for a few more minutes."

They walked up Madison Avenue together, chatting about nothing in particular. Tommi actually caught herself slowing down her usual Manhattan march to more of a stroll, pausing to look into store windows—anything to draw out the pleasant moment. All too soon, though, they reached the street entrance to the parking garage where Tommi's family kept their cars.

"Here we are," she said reluctantly.

Alex spun her around, putting his other hand around her waist. "Are you sure you have to go?" he wheedled.

"I'm sure," Tommi said with a smile. "Sorry. Maybe we can get together over the weekend? I don't have a show or anything."

"Sounds like a plan. I'll text you later." He leaned forward to kiss her. She kissed him back, then suddenly pulled away.

"Hey," she said. "You said your aunt's up on Eighty-Eighth Street, right? I could drop you off if you want—it's not that far out of my way."

"Really? Cool." He kissed her on the tip of the nose. "Thanks."

Tommi smiled. Okay, so the slight detour would make her even later. Oh well. Kate would understand.

"Sorry!" Tommi rushed into the barn. Kate was in the aisle, picking out a horse's hooves. "I know I'm way late. I just totally lost track of time."

Now that she was here, she felt a little guilty for blowing off their meeting time. Not that she'd trade a minute of her morning for anything. The more time she spent with Alex, the more time she wanted to spend with him. It seemed as if they never ran out of things to talk about. And if they did? Well, talking wasn't the only thing she enjoyed doing with him.

In any case, she was here now. No point stressing about it, especially since Kate looked as if she'd been keeping herself busy, as usual.

Kate set down the horse's left front and straightened up. "It's okay," she said. "I got your text. Was traffic bad?"

"Sort of." Tommi glanced at the horse, a fancy bay mare belonging to one of the adults. "What are you doing?"

"Mrs. Walsh just finished her lesson. Javier was busy dragging the indoor, so I offered to untack and groom."

"Well, you'd better let one of the other guys finish that before Jamie catches you."

She was mostly joking. But just then Jamie himself rounded the corner and spotted them.

"Kate," he said with a sigh. "Isn't this supposed to be your day off?"

"It's totally my fault, Jamie," Tommi put in with a rueful smile. "I asked Kate to meet me here and then I was late, and—"

"It's all right, Tommi." Jamie didn't even glance at her. He was gazing at Kate with a serious, vaguely worried expression on his face. "Can I talk to you for a sec, Kate?"

"Sure," Kate said in a small voice. She shot Tommi a glance. "Be right back."

"Okay." Tommi watched them disappear into Jamie's office a couple of doors down from the tack room. What was that all about? Sure, everyone knew about Kate being banned from the barn on her day off. It was kind of a running joke. But Jamie hadn't been joking around just now. Was something going on with Kate that she didn't know about?

Whatever. She figured it was none of her business—if Kate wanted to share, she would. Mrs. Walsh's mare seemed to be groomed and ready, so Tommi stuck her back in her stall, then continued down the aisle to look in on Legs.

But the bay gelding's stall was empty. Elliot was sweeping the aisle nearby and saw her looking.

"He's outside," he called, leaning on his broom. "Jamie didn't think you were coming to ride today, so he said put him out to let him stretch his legs."

"Oh. Okay, thanks." Tommi thought about going to find the horse in his paddock, but decided against it. She didn't want to keep Kate waiting yet again.

As she wandered back down the aisle, she heard Jamie's voice drifting out of his office. ". . . and I'm really starting to get concerned about how hard you've been working lately," he was saying. "If you keep it up, you're liable to burn out. Trust me, I've been there."

Kate said something in response, but her voice was too soft for Tommi to make out the words. Just as well. She definitely hadn't meant to eavesdrop. Feeling guilty, she hurried quickly past the office door so she wouldn't hear any more.

"Thanks so much for the ride, Stacie!" Zara said with a big, cheerful smile. She shut the door of Zac's second-favorite Corvette ragtop a little harder than necessary, smirking as she saw her cousin wince.

"Yeah, you're welcome. Bye," Stacie said in a voice that sounded like it was coming from the bottom of a sewer pipe. When you tossed in her pasty skin, unwashed hair, and the red eyes behind her shades, she was pretty much the dictionary definition of a bad hangover.

Throwing the car into gear, she pulled out. Zara grinned and watched until the convertible disappeared around the first bend in Pelham Lane's long, winding drive. Served her right. The girl's constant partying was really getting on Zara's nerves. Didn't she ever take a break? Zara was starting to think the prissy nanny type she'd been expecting would've been easier to deal with after all.

She headed into the barn and found Tommi sitting on the bench just inside the main entrance, scratching Jamie's fat old bulldog behind the ears. "Hey," Zara said. "What's up?"

"Not much," Tommi said. "You have a lesson today or something?"

"No." Zara shrugged. "Nothing going on back in the city, so I figured I'd come out and hack or something."

"Oh." Just then Tommi glanced down the aisle and stood up.

Following her gaze, Zara saw Jamie and Kate emerging from Jamie's office. The trainer spotted her in turn and walked over.

"Zara," he said. "I didn't know you were coming out today."

"Just call me Miss Spontaneous," Zara said. "I decided I felt like a ride."

Jamie frowned. "I see. Well, Keeper lost a shoe in turnout last night, and you scheduled a schooling ride for Ellie today and Joy already worked her pretty hard."

"Oops, I forgot about that." Zara shrugged. "Guess it's not my lucky day."

Jamie checked his watch. "Look, I can find you something else to ride if you like," he said. "But it'll have to wait. I'm already keeping Mrs. Walsh waiting for her lesson. Come find me afterward if you want."

"I have a better idea," Tommi spoke up as the trainer hurried off. "Why don't you come tack shopping with us?" She gestured to herself and Kate.

"Really?" Zara was surprised. Sure, the other juniors had been acting a bit friendlier lately. At least off and on. But they still weren't exactly BFFs.

"Sure. Have you been to the big tack store near here? It's actually pretty good." Tommi shrugged. "Like I said, we're heading over there anyway, so you're welcome to join us."

"Sounds like a plan." Zara glanced at Kate, who hadn't said anything. She was staring off into space, not even seeming to be paying attention. "Actually, I could use a new jacket," Zara told Tommi. "The one I bought at that last show is a little too big."

"Then let's go," Tommi said. "I'll drive."

Half an hour later the three of them were browsing through the apparel section of the spacious, well-stocked tack shop. "You were right, this place is pretty cool," Zara told Tommi, examining a white-on-white striped Van Teal shirt, then glancing around the hushed, dark-wood interior of the store. "Who knew you could find such nice stuff out in the boonies?"

Tommi was digging through a rack of show shirts marked NEW ARRIVALS. "I know, right?" she said. "It's super convenient to the barn. Most of us do all our shopping here."

She tossed a pale green windowpane-checked shirt into her basket and moved on to the next rack. Zara followed, picking up a pastel yellow Marigold shirt.

"How's this color on me?" she asked, holding up the shirt. "It would go great with my dark brown jacket."

"Looks good. That color really works with your skin," Tommi said, glancing up. "Plus my motto is, you can never have too many show shirts."

Zara grinned. "Can't argue with that."

She dropped the shirt into her own basket, atop the new schooling helmet, several pairs of fun funky-colored boot socks, and two pairs of breeches she'd already picked out. Then she glanced over at Kate, who was checking out a rack of gloves nearby.

"Finding anything good?" Zara asked, wandering over to take a look herself. "Hey, you don't even have a basket."

"I don't really need anything." Kate looked up with that wimpy little smile of hers. "I'm just browsing today."

"Whatever floats your boat." Zara shrugged and turned to examine the gloves. She wasn't much of a browser herself. Shopping was a lot more fun when you came home with lots of pretty new toys.

Then again, it was obvious just from looking at her that Kate probably couldn't afford to shop at a place like this. Why else would she bust her butt working at the barn all the time?

Oh, well. Too bad, so sad. At least maybe she could live vicariously through Zara and Tommi.

"Ooh, those look nice," Zara said, noticing that Kate had just picked up a pair of black Roeckl gloves. "I need a new pair of show gloves."

She grabbed another pair of the same gloves and pulled them on. The material was buttery soft.

"They look comfortable," Kate said, watching.

"They are. Go ahead—try them on and see." Zara rolled her eyes as she saw Kate hesitate. Yeah, that pretty much confirmed what she'd been thinking earlier. Even the idea of trying on a pair of fifty-dollar show gloves sent Kate into a panic. "Who cares if you're not really shopping today? There's no law against trying stuff on."

"I guess." Kate slipped the gloves on over her long, slim hands. They fit like a—well, like a glove. Duh. Zara suddenly got where that saying came from.

"Nice, huh?" She flexed her fingers to test out the pair she was wearing. "No trouble handling the reins in these, even if you're riding in a pelham."

"Yeah." Kate pulled off the gloves. "They're really nice."

Carefully hooking the gloves together, she hung them on the rack and then picked up a pair of cheap work gloves. Zara peeled off one of the Roeckls, still watching Kate. Here the girl was shopping with her and Tommi, two people who could buy out the entire store if they felt like it. And she wasn't even hinting for them to buy her something. Impressive.

Not to mention way different from most of the people Zara had ever known, at least the ones pretending to be her friends. If there was one thing she'd learned to despise over the years, it was a user. And Kate seemed to be pretty much the opposite of one. Sure, the girl was way too quiet, and maybe a little prissy. But she and Tommi might be the closest thing Zara had to friends at her new barn so far. That was worth something.

Zara dropped her pair of Roeckls into her basket, then

— 141 —

grabbed the ones Kate had tried on. "I can't stand to see anyone shop and not buy anything," she announced, tossing the second pair on top of the first. "Think I'd better fix that. You're getting these."

"What?" Kate looked alarmed. "No, seriously, Zara. I can't afford—"

"Forget it," Zara said. "They're yours. My treat."

It was actually kind of fun ignoring the other girl's feeble protests while she and Tommi continued shopping. And even more fun to see the look on Kate's face when Zara handed over the gloves as they left the store after checking out. Yeah, okay. Now she got why her mom and all those other Hollywood stars liked doing charity work. Doing something nice for someone, for no particular reason at all? Kind of awesome.

TWELVE

On Saturday morning Kate pulled into her usual spot in the Pelham Lane parking lot. Her car let out a funny little wheeze as she cut the engine, making her wince. She really hoped there wasn't something wrong with it. No way could she afford a mechanic's bill right now, and she hated asking her father for help.

Kate climbed out of her car and glanced toward the barn, tempted to go in and see if Joy needed her to do anything before she took off for Happy Acres. But Fitz would be here any minute to meet her. Besides, she didn't want to risk another little talk from Jamie like the one yesterday. What had gotten into him, anyway? She hadn't been acting any differently than normal lately—well, unless you counted that pathetic ride she'd given Fable in their last eq class. Could that be why he was upset with her? Maybe he thought she needed to spend less time working at the barn and more time working on her eq so she wouldn't embarrass him again at the next show.

She forgot about that as she saw Fitz's cherry-red convertible race up the drive, sending gravel flying everywhere. He didn't bother to park, just throwing it into neutral behind Kate's car.

"Sorry I'm late," he said, hopping out without bothering to open the car door. "I actually left like twenty minutes before I normally would, but there was an accident on the bridge."

"It's okay, I just got here," Kate said.

He grabbed her hand and pulled her in for a quick kiss. Then he hurried around to the passenger side of his car. "Your chariot awaits," he said, opening the door with a flourish.

Soon they were heading back down the drive. Kate noticed that Fitz was taking it a lot slower than he had on the way in. Was that for her benefit?

"So how was your girls' day out thing yesterday?" he asked.

"Fine. Fun, actually." Kate felt a rush of mixed feelings when she thought back to yesterday's shopping trip. Hanging out with Tommi was always fun, but Kate had been surprised by how well Zara had fit in. Plus Kate always loved window-shopping at that place, even if she could only dream of affording anything bigger than a hoof pick there.

But then there was the thing with those gloves. Guilt gnawed at her every time she thought about that. Why hadn't she protested harder when Zara had offered to buy them for her? It wasn't like her old show gloves were totally worn out yet. Then again, Zara seemed like the kind of person who didn't take "No thanks" as an answer.

"You okay?" Fitz glanced over as he coasted to a stop at the bottom of the driveway. "You just went all quiet."

"Sorry. Um, turn right here."

Fitz pulled out onto the quiet country highway. "So?" he said. "What's got you looking all emo all of a sudden?"

"It's nothing," Kate said. "Just, um . . ." She caught herself about to concoct some lame excuse about not getting enough sleep or something. It was pretty obvious that Fitz was trying hard with her. If she wanted things to work between them, she needed to meet him halfway. At least start trusting him about the little stuff. Otherwise, what was the point?

"Um, it's just that Zara ended up tagging along to the tack store," she said. "She showed up at the barn as we were getting ready to leave, and Tommi invited her."

"Ouch." Fitz shot her a look. "Since when are Tommi and Zara friends? I thought they bitched each other out every chance they got."

"No, they're over that. I think." Kate shrugged. "Anyway, she was really nice yesterday."

"So what's the problem?"

Kate glanced over at him. "I was looking at these gloves, and she decided to buy them for me."

"And?" Fitz said expectantly.

"And they were really expensive. Like fifty bucks."

Fitz laughed. "And you're stressing about it? Listen, Kate, don't bother. Zara probably drops more than that tipping her hairdresser. I'm sure she didn't think twice about it, and neither should you."

Kate forced a smile. She knew he was trying to make her feel better, but it was having the opposite effect. Sometimes it really sucked, feeling so different from her friends at Pelham

Lane. Like being the only one riding a Shetland in a hack class full of warmbloods, and knowing she was stuck with that shaggy little pony forever thanks to forces beyond her control.

She snapped out of it as she realized their next turn was coming up. "Take a left up there by the crooked tree," she said, pointing. "The farm's a couple of miles down that road."

"So what's this friend of yours like, anyway?" Fitz asked as he spun the wheel. "She a good rider?"

"Sure, I guess." Kate hesitated, wondering how to translate Natalie into terms Fitz would understand. "I mean, she's pretty bold and gets the job done. But she's never had the chance to train with someone like Jamie, so she doesn't have the same kind of, you know, show-ring polish that we're used to at Pelham Lane."

"Okay," Fitz said. "Should be interesting."

His tone was neutral, even light. But Kate felt her nerves flare again. Had it been a mistake to let him come? Oh well, too late now.

Soon they were turning into the bumpy gravel drive. Kate grinned nostalgically as she spotted a fat gray pony grazing behind the patched-together but functional wood-and-wire fencing of the front pasture.

"Look, it's Elmo!" she exclaimed, pointing. "I've been afraid to ask Nat if he's still alive—he must be like pushing forty by now! He was one of the first ponies I ever rode."

"Cool." Fitz grinned, glancing at the pony. "I can totally picture it—you as a little kid with long, skinny legs riding some evil little monster pony across a field at top speed."

Kate laughed. "Yeah, that was pretty much how I learned

to ride after the first few lessons," she said. "Elmo was pretty old even back then, but he definitely had an evil side. He was a great teacher, though."

They rounded the curve and came within sight of the barn. The parking area between the barn and the equipment shed was jammed with cars, minivans, and a few bumper-pull trailers. Horses, ponies, kids, parents, and dogs were milling around everywhere. Beyond the barn, Kate could see a few riders already warming up in the big outdoor sand ring.

"Wow, the place looks exactly the same," she said as she took it all in. "Well, except the flowers by the barn doors. They must've put those there to decorate for the show."

"Cool place," Fitz said as he squeezed his car into a free spot between an old Chevy pickup and the wall of the shed. "Very homey."

Kate shot him a look to see if he was being sarcastic. But he was looking around with what appeared to be real interest.

"Yeah," she said. "Come on, let's go find Nat."

She led the way toward the barn. A stout woman was just coming out as they neared the door. She was in her fifties with a long, gray ponytail.

"Katie!" she exclaimed, rushing over to envelop Kate in her plump, sunburned arms. "You made it! Nat said you might come. It's so good to see you again, darling. How come you never come to visit us?"

"I've been meaning to, Mrs. Tanner." Kate was a little breathless from the barn owner's enthusiastic hug. "It's just been a really busy summer."

Just then a pair of preteen girls raced over. One was

dressed in yellowish-beige schooling breeches and a pale blue polo shirt with a cardboard number flapping on a string tied around her waist. The other was in jeans and a T-shirt.

"Mrs. T, Roscoe won't let us catch him!" the first girl cried, sounding frantic. "And I'm supposed to be in the walk-trot equitation class, and I can't even find the saddle I usually use! I think someone else took it!"

"Yeah. Plus Roscoe rolled in the mud, and Marc said we can't ride in the show unless the horses are totally clean," the second girl offered.

Mrs. Tanner rolled her eyes. "Settle down, girls. I'll help you catch Roscoe. And you should know better than to listen to that son of mine." She shot Kate an apologetic look. "I'd better go deal with this, darling."

"Sure," Kate said. "Um, but wait, is Natalie around?"

"Pretty sure she's in the barn helping the kids tack up." The barn owner waved, then hurried off after the two younger girls.

Fitz was peering into the barn. It was a long center-aisle setup with a dozen stalls and bad lighting. Horses and ponies were cross-tied all up and down the aisle, with kids running here and there grooming, tacking up, and adjusting their own clothes.

"Looks like an obstacle course in there," Fitz joked.

"Yeah. It's always a little crazy at these shows," Kate said. "Come on, follow me."

She spotted Natalie halfway down the aisle, standing in the open doorway of an unoccupied stall. She had a bridle draped over each shoulder and a hoofpick in her hand. "Get over here,

Jenny!" she was hollering. "You can't show unless you pick out your pony's feet, you hear me?"

"But he'll kick me!" a little girl whined as she ducked under a sleepy-looking pinto's nose and hurried over. She was dressed in a short-sleeved button-down shirt and what appeared to be a pair of black leggings. Her paddock boots were dusty, and stray blond hairs drifted from under the edge of her plastic schooling helmet. Back in the day, Kate wouldn't have thought twice about the girl's turnout. These shows were supposed to be casual, after all—a way for lesson kids to get their first taste of showing in a supportive atmosphere. And they were perfect for that.

But now she couldn't help seeing it through Fitz's eyes—all of it. She glanced around at all the secondhand schooling breeches in wild colors, the hodgepodge of shirts and jackets, the mostly unbraided manes, and barely a hairnet in sight. What must he be thinking about the whole scene?

"He won't kick you. I promise." Natalie stuck the pick into the girl's hand, gave her a shove in the direction of one of the ponies cross-tied farther down the aisle, then spun around. "Where's Frannie? She's supposed to . . ."

Her voice trailed off as she spotted Kate. Kate smiled tentatively. "Hey," she said. "It's me."

"Katie!" Natalie grabbed her in a hug. "You made it!"

"I said I would, right?" Kate hugged her back. Just like that, their fight was over. It was always that way with Nat. She had a temper, but she wasn't the type to stay mad for long. She didn't have the attention span.

Natalie pushed Kate away when she spotted Fitz. "So who's this?" she asked with obvious interest.

Fitz stepped forward. "Fitz Hall," he said. "Nice to meet you, Natalie. Kate's told me all about you."

"Really? Because she's pretty much been keeping you a big, bad secret." Natalie smirked as she took his outstretched hand. "No, seriously, she's mentioned you, but you know how our Katie can be." She laughed. "But now I get it. No wonder she wants to keep you all to yourself. Lucky girl."

Kate felt her face go red, but Fitz just laughed. "No way, I'm the lucky one." He put an arm around Kate's shoulders. "I mean, just look at her, right?"

"Sweet," Nat declared. Then she grabbed Kate's arm and checked her watch. "Whoa. I'm way behind—I should be bridling Flame right now."

"Flame?" Fitz said. "Is that your horse?"

Nat shrugged. "Well, he's not technically mine, but I'm the only one riding him right now. He's this new horse the Tanners got off the track. Kind of a nut, but we're making progress. Anyway, I said I'd take him in a couple of classes today, see how he does. So I'd better go finish getting him ready."

"Want some help?" Kate offered.

"Sure." Nat flashed her a grateful smile. "Grab a brush and come with me."

"Here's Legs." Tommi stopped in front of the gelding's stall.

"Cool." Alex watched as she fed Legs a treat. "So this is the beast who's going to launch your fabulous career as a horse pro, huh?"

"Knock on wood," Tommi said with a smile. She was having

fun showing Alex around the barn. So far he'd met Jamie, Joy, Toccata, several other horses, and most of the barn dogs.

Just then she heard the clatter of hooves. Glancing down the aisle, she saw Javier leading Summer's horse toward the wash stalls. Summer was wandering along behind them, peeling off her crochet-back gloves.

As the groom disappeared around the corner, Summer spotted Tommi and Alex. "Hi, Tommi," she said, sizing up Alex with naked interest as she hurried over. "What's up?"

"Not much," Tommi said. "Just showing Alex around. Alex, this is Summer. Summer, my friend Alex."

"Friend?" Summer said.

Alex stepped up behind Tommi and wrapped both arms around her waist. "Yeah," he said, nuzzling her neck. "We're really *good* friends."

"Oh." Summer's face dropped. "Nice to meet you. I'd better go check on my horse."

Tommi waited until Summer scurried off to laugh. "That wasn't very nice," she chided jokingly. "She was ready to jump your bones."

"I know, I was kind of scared." Alex grinned. "Now come on—are you going to teach me to ride, or what?"

"Sure, let's go." Tommi led him to a stall farther down the aisle.

Alex looked dubious when he saw the slightly swaybacked chestnut dozing inside. "This is the horse I'm going to ride?" he said. "He looks kind of small."

"That's Sir. He's not as tall as my horses, but he's plenty big enough, trust me," Tommi said. Sir belonged to one of the barn's adult clients, who allowed Jamie to use the steady older gelding as a lesson and lease horse for newer riders. He was leased out to a pre-children's rider this summer, but the kid was on vacation with her family in Maine this week, and so Jamie had given Tommi permission to use Sir for Alex's riding lesson.

She tacked up quickly, then led Sir and Alex outside to the flatwork ring, which was unoccupied at the moment. The sweet old gelding stood quietly at the mounting block as Tommi tossed the reins over his head and checked the girth.

"Put your left foot in the stirrup and grab a hunk of his mane," Tommi instructed Alex. "Then swing your—oh, okay. You've got it."

Alex vaulted on, landing in the saddle with a thump. "Okay," he said with a grin. "Now what? Do I just say 'Hi-ho, Silver!' and give him a kick?"

"No!" Tommi said quickly. "I mean, please don't. Sir might look quiet, and he is, but he's also pretty well tuned. He'll walk on if you just give him a little nudge with your heels."

"Got it." Alex grabbed the reins and poked the horse in the gut with both heels. Sir lifted his head, then stepped off.

"Good boy," Tommi told the horse. "Walk on." Then she glanced at Alex. "You're not holding the reins right," she said. "Turn your hands like this." She lifted her own hands to demonstrate. "And keep your heels down."

He adjusted his grip and jammed his heels down. "Got it. When do I get to canter?"

Tommi laughed. "You haven't even learned to trot yet."

"What's to learn? Come on, boy—let's trot!" Alex gave Sir a kick.

The horse flicked an ear back, seeming uncertain, but broke into a slow, lumbering trot. Tommi winced as she saw Alex's seat bounce out of the saddle and slam down again at the next stride. She'd sort of forgotten that Sir was famous for two things—his sweet temperament and his jarring trot. He was the one Jamie used to test the cocky advanced beginners who were convinced that they had the sitting trot down.

"Push your heels down!" Tommi called. "Pull on the reins and he'll slow back down to a walk."

Alex didn't answer. She wasn't sure he'd even heard her. He was still bouncing around in the saddle, and as Sir bent to follow the curve of the ring fence, Alex's left foot flew out of the stirrup.

"Whoa!" he cried, slipping to the side. Dropping the reins, he grabbed the front of the saddle to keep himself in place.

"Easy, boy!" Tommi called to the horse. "Walk, Sir. Walk on."

The horse slowed immediately, giving Alex the chance to haul himself back into position and jam his foot back in the stirrup. "Thanks," he said with a sheepish grin. "This riding stuff's harder than it looks in the movies."

"Yeah." Tommi couldn't help smirking. "Now you know why I take all those lessons."

He laughed good-naturedly. "Guess so," he agreed. "Can I blame it on being totally distracted by my hot riding teacher?"

"Nice try. Want to give it another go?"

"Sure. Maybe a little slower this time."

Tommi smiled, glad that he was being such a good sport. A lot of guys who came out to ride with their girlfriends started off just like he had—convinced that riding was no big deal, that all you had to do was sit there. Most of them never got any farther than that. But she already knew Alex wasn't like most guys.

By the end of half an hour or so, Alex was looking pretty competent at the walk and learning to post Sir's trot. He was pretty athletic, and once he started listening to Tommi's instructions, he learned fast.

"That was fun," he said as he watched Tommi untack Sir in the cross-ties. "Maybe we can do it again sometime."

Tommi grinned. "You might not say that tomorrow," she said. "You'll be sore in muscles you didn't even know existed. Trust me on that."

Alex didn't answer. He was staring down the aisle. Following his gaze, Tommi saw that Zara had just appeared around the corner. She'd unbuttoned her tight polo shirt so her cleavage was on full display, and at first Tommi assumed that was what had caught Alex's attention. He was a guy, after all.

Then he glanced over at her. "Isn't that Zac Trask's daughter?" he said. "I'd love to meet her."

Zara was already wandering over. "Hey," she said, her green eyes sweeping up and down Alex's body. "So you found another hottie to bring out to the barn, huh, Tommi?"

Tommi wondered if that meant she had something going with Grant. She hadn't mentioned it on their shopping trip yesterday, but then again, Tommi hadn't asked.

"This is Alex," she said. "Alex, Zara Trask."

"I know. It's cool to meet you, Zara—I'm a big fan of your dad's," Alex said eagerly. "Tommi told me you rode here. That's cool. So does your dad ever come to watch you ride?"

"He's not going to show up today, if that's what you're wondering." Zara rolled her eyes. "He's in Europe for most of the summer."

"Oh, I know. I read all about it on his Facebook fan page." Alex laughed self-consciously. "I know, I know, totally geeky, right? But I can't help it—the guy's a genius. But I guess you know that if he's your own father!"

"Yeah," Zara said dryly. "Total genius."

Tommi finished grooming Sir as Alex continued to shoot questions and comments at Zara. It was pretty obvious that Zara was getting kind of annoyed, but Alex didn't seem to notice. In fact, he was pretty much inviting himself to hang out with Zac once he was back in the country.

Okay, obnoxious. But hey, the guy was a total music freak. So he was geeked about maybe meeting his idol. So what? Tommi wasn't going to hold something like that against him when everything else about him was so amazing. It was actually kind of refreshing to find out that he might have a flaw or two. Because up until now, he'd seemed so perfect that she'd almost started to wonder if he could possibly be for real.

THIRTEEN

"So this is him," Natalie said. "My boy. What do you think?"

She'd just led Kate and Fitz outside to the hitching rail behind the barn. A tall, thin chestnut gelding was tied there. Kate estimated the horse at 16'3" at least, which was kind of surprising. Happy Acres specialized in kids' lessons, and it was rare to find a horse on the place that was much over 15'2", aside from a couple of Belgians used for carriage rides.

"He's a tall one," Fitz said. Kate guessed that the horse's height might be the only thing he felt safe commenting on. He probably wasn't so impressed with the gelding's ribbiness or his rough, dirty coat.

But Kate *was* kind of impressed. She'd been expecting some kind of weedy little downhill sprinter type with big ankles and an upside-down neck. But this horse actually had pretty good structure under his unkempt exterior.

"He's cute," Kate told Natalie. "I can see why you call him Flame. His color's really flashy."

"Oh, it's not because of that." Natalie hoisted the saddle she was carrying onto the rail. "His racing name's Open Flame. It works in more ways than one, actually—he's pretty hot to ride." She grabbed one of the brushes Kate had picked up in the tack room on their way out of the barn. "Come on, help me knock the dirt off him."

In this case, that wasn't just a figure of speech. It looked as if Flame had been rolling in the mud—a lot—and probably hadn't had a bath since he'd left the track. Kate set to work with a curry, loosening the ground-in dirt as best she could.

"Good boy," she murmured as the horse twisted his head to stare at her curiously. Her fingers were itching to reach up and start pulling his mane, which was uneven and a little long. But there probably wasn't time for that, plus she wasn't sure Nat would appreciate it. She'd probably think it was just one of those habits Kate had picked up at her "snobby big-time show barn."

"Wish we had the vacuum," Fitz said, coughing as he raised a cloud of dust with his curry.

Natalie shot him a look. "Ha-ha, very funny. Kate didn't tell me you were a comedian."

"He's not joking," Kate said quickly, wanting to head off any potential tension between Nat and Fitz. "Jamie's got this, like, special horse vacuum. It's really helpful for getting all the ground-in dirt and loose hair off a horse."

"Seriously?" Nat looked kind of suspicious, as if she still didn't quite believe them. "Okay, guess he had to spend all that money his rich-ass clients are paying him on something."

Kate winced, hoping Fitz didn't take offense. But when she glanced over at him, he was grinning.

"True," he said. "But he totally refuses to shell out for a

pinball machine, no matter how much I beg. Says it'll spook the horses."

That made Nat laugh, then start chattering about how Flame had spooked at something or other the last time she rode him. Kate let out a silent breath, grateful for once that Fitz didn't take anything too seriously.

The horse still wasn't exactly up to Pelham Lane standards when Nat started tacking up, but he looked better. Kate could tell that his bright chestnut coat was healthy, and would probably shine like a copper penny with just a little more elbow grease. Not to mention how nice his four white socks and big, symmetrical blaze would look if they were shampooed and chalked.

"Wish me luck!" Natalie said, breaking into Kate's thoughts. The saddle and bridle were on, and Nat was leading the horse over toward the sturdy wooden mounting block just outside the grass paddock that served as a warm-up ring. Fitz held Flame's head while Natalie swung aboard.

"Good luck," Kate said as her friend rode off through the gate. There were only a few kids on ponies in there, clustered around a woman Kate didn't recognize. One of the barn's newer instructors, maybe? Kate felt a pang as she realized how much had changed since she'd left. A few short years ago, she would have known everyone at this show. Now, aside from Nat and the Tanners, she only recognized a handful of faces. Even many of the horses and ponies were new to her.

As she stepped forward to join Fitz, who was leaning on the rail, Kate shifted her gaze to Natalie. She'd just kicked Flame forward. He tossed his head and skittered sideways, then stepped into a flat-kneed, ground-covering trot.

"Wow," Kate said, impressed anew. "He's a really nice mover."

"You mean Mr. Ribs? You think so?" Fitz sounded dubious. "I mean, yeah, I guess compared to the fat little ponies."

"No, seriously." Kate kept her eyes on the horse. "I already noticed his conformation was pretty good—great shoulder, level topline, just good angles all around. He could be a real diamond in the rough in the right hands."

"Like yours?" Fitz glanced over with a smile.

"I was thinking of Jamie, actually." Kate watched as Nat struggled to slow the horse down, yanking on the reins and growling as Flame tossed his head in protest. "If this guy can jump at all, I bet Jamie could turn him into an A-quality hunter with just a little bit of work. All he needs is some weight and TLC and good training."

Fitz shrugged, not looking fully convinced. "If you say so," he said. "But Natalie said he's pretty hot, right? Maybe too hot to make a hunter."

Kate didn't respond to that. She already had her doubts about how hot this horse really was. So far he wasn't giving Nat much real trouble, though it was clear he didn't know much beyond his track training.

"He's not sure what to do with the bit yet," she said as Nat finally wrestled the horse back to a jiggy walk. "If it were up to me, I'd just let him go long and low for a while until he relaxes and learns he can trust his rider."

"Sounds good, Jamie Junior," Fitz said with a laugh. "Maybe you can give Natalie a few lessons."

"No way." Kate shuddered at the thought. "She already thinks I'm a know-it-all since I moved to Jamie's barn. If I tried to tell her how to train her new project, she'd probably bite my head off."

Fitz looked surprised. "Really? But she must realize what an awesome rider you are, right?"

Kate just shrugged. "Anyway, it's too bad," she said, talking more to herself than to Fitz now. "That horse could really be something special."

"You know, maybe you're right." Fitz turned to watch Natalie ride past again. "I mean, I didn't really see it at first. But you've got a great eye, Kate." He reached over and gave her a quick squeeze on the shoulder.

"Thanks." She smiled at him, her shoulder tingling. She hadn't been sure it was a good idea for him to come today. To say the least. But now she was glad he was here.

Soon it was time for Nat and her mount to head into the show ring. They were entered in a division called Beginner Horse, for green horses and those new to showing, consisting of three classes: walk-trot, walk-trot-canter, and jumping a course of two-foot fences. When she was riding at Happy Acres, Kate had taken countless potential lesson horses and ponies in the same division for their first show-ring experience, fresh from the auction or Craigslist.

Nat and Flame rode in along with six or seven others, mostly tween kids on bratty-looking ponies. Everyone walked along on the rail until Mr. Tanner arrived with his portable microphone to start the class.

"Riders, you're now being judged," he said, perching the speaker on a fence post. "Walk please—all walk."

It was kind of a disaster from the start. In the walk-trot

class, Flame's stride was so much longer that he ended up lapping everyone else in the ring. That seemed to excite him—racetrack flashback, Kate figured—and he just kept getting faster and more strung out. In the walk-trot-canter class, he leaped into a near-gallop and almost ran over a couple of ponies as Nat wrestled to slow him down.

Still, everyone survived. Kate half expected Nat to bow out of the jumping—that was what Kate herself would have done under the circumstances—but no. She went in, executed a lopsided opening circle at a skittering half trot, half canter, and aimed the horse at the first fence.

"Yikes," Fitz said as Flame left from a super long spot.

Luckily the fence was small enough that it wasn't a problem, though the horse's hind foot clunked the rail. That spooked him, sending him spurting forward so quickly that he almost crashed right through the next jump in the line. He noticed it just in time and planted his feet, skidding to a near stop before Natalie let out a shout and booted him forward. He sprang over the fence with his head in the air and a startled look in his eyes.

Kate could hardly stand to watch as Nat manhandled the gelding around the rest of the course. But again, everyone survived. And Natalie was actually grinning as she rode out of the ring.

"Wow, that was an adventure," she said, riding over to where Kate and Fitz were standing. "I don't know, riding a hot horse like this guy kind of makes normal horses seem boring."

Fitz chuckled politely, and Kate forced a smile as she reached out to give the sweaty gelding a pat. Okay, so he hadn't exactly clocked around like a children's hunter. That didn't mean he was "hot," as Nat seemed to think. Just green and confused.

But she wasn't about to say so. Not now, when she and Nat were finally back on track.

🐎

"Wow!" Dani let out a wolf whistle as Zara wandered into the tack room. "Hello, sexy! You're sure not dressed for mucking stalls."

She and Marissa were lounging on the bandage trunk sharing a bag of Doritos. Zara glanced down at her low-cut beaded cami and short shorts.

"What, this old thing?" she joked. "Yeah, actually I kind of have a date. Lucky I forgot this in my tack trunk after the last show so I didn't have to go in boots and breeches." She shrugged. "Although some guys dig that look, I guess."

Marissa grinned, her gossip radar zeroing in on Zara. "A date? Spill it!" she demanded. "Who is he? Anyone we know?"

"Remember that guy Grant, from the Hounds Hollow party?"

"You mean that preppy friend of Tommi's?" Dani said. "The one who was all over you in the pool?"

"That's the guy." Zara smiled. "He's kind of been after me ever since."

"Lucky," Marissa declared. "He's totally hot. Where do I sign up for next dibs on Tommi's leftovers? Because I wouldn't mind getting to know that guy she brought out today. Did you guys get a load of him?"

Leftovers? Um, so *not*. But Zara was in too good a mood to let the other girl's stupid comment bother her.

"Anyway," she said, "Grant called and wanted to see me, and I wasn't sure I was in the mood. So I told him we could only get together if he came up here." She smiled as she remembered how quickly that return text had come. Okay, so she usually liked her guys a little wilder, a little edgier, a little more dangerous. But it was always nice to be wanted. "Guess he really wanted to see me, because we're going to the diner. He's picking me up out front in like—" She checked her watch. "Oops, ten minutes ago. Got to go, girls."

"Don't do anything I wouldn't do!" Dani sang out as Zara hurried out of the tack room.

"No promises," Zara called back over her shoulder with a grin.

A short while later she and Grant were sitting at one of the tables along the diner's plate-glass front windows. The place was pretty crowded, even though it was almost 3:00 p.m.

"I'm glad this worked out," Grant said as he reached for his water glass. "I was afraid you guys might be away at another show or something."

"Nope, off week." Zara spotted their waitress making her way toward them along the narrow alleyway between tables, a loaded tray balanced against one shoulder. "Awesome, food's here. I'm starving. Rode three horses this morning."

"Really? I thought you only had two," Grant said. "That new one you were talking about, and the one you brought with you from California."

"Impressive," Zara said. "Most guys don't pay much attention to what I say. Especially when I'm wearing something like this." She leaned forward a little and shook her shoulders.

She wasn't wearing a bra, so the movement resulted in significant jigglage.

The waitress, an older woman with gray-streaked red hair piled atop her head in a messy bun, shot Zara a look of weary disdain as she dropped a couple of plates in front of her and Grant. "Anything else, kids?" she asked, snapping her gum.

"We're good, thanks." Grant sounded as polite as ever, even though his face had gone bright red and he was carefully avoiding looking directly at Zara.

Zara grinned at him as the waitress hurried off. "You're way too easy to mess with," she told him, reaching for her burger. "Anyway, the third horse I rode was one of Jamie's sales ponies. He needed someone short to hack it, and I was there."

She kept her voice casual, still surprised and kind of pleased that the trainer had asked her. That definitely wouldn't have happened a couple of weeks ago. Not that she cared that much. But hey, it was something.

But Grant wasn't looking at her anyway. "Aren't those people from your barn?" he asked.

Twisting around in her seat, Zara saw that Fitz and Kate had just entered and were standing by the hostess stand. "Yeah, but that's weird," she said. "I was hanging around the barn most of the day, and I didn't see either of them there."

A moment later a different waitress grabbed a couple of menus out of the bin by the door and gestured. Fitz grabbed Kate by the hand and followed the waitress down the aisle. When they neared Zara and Grant, Fitz grinned.

"Hey guys, what's up?" he said, stopping at the end of their table. "Were you at the barn?"

"Yeah, I was," Zara replied. "Didn't see you two there."

"We weren't." Fitz glanced at Kate, who was smiling her wimpy little smile and not saying anything. "We went to watch a show at Kate's old barn. But we left a little early because we were both starving."

"Cool. Want to join us?" Grant said.

Zara shot him a look. Okay, so she was getting used to Kate. Maybe even starting to like her, sort of. And Fitz was always fun, of course. But she'd thought the whole point of Grant driving all the way up from the city was to be with her. Was he just being Mr. Super Polite, or what?

"Sounds like fun, but can we do it some other time?" Fitz grinned. "Gotta admit, I've been dying to get Kate to myself all day." He wrapped one long arm around her shoulders and squeezed.

"I hear you, man. Totally. Catch you later." Grant lifted a hand as the pair hurried off after their waitress. Then he picked up his burger and glanced at Zara. "Cute couple, huh? Like something out of an ad, all tall and thin and blond."

"I guess." Zara watched as Fitz and Kate sat down at a table in the next section. She almost wished they'd ended up a little closer so she could eavesdrop. What the hell did the two of them talk about, anyway? When she'd first arrived at Pelham Lane, everyone had warned her that Fitz was a total player. But it didn't look that way to her. He really seemed to be into Kate, even if Zara couldn't figure out why. "Maybe skinny chicks just turn him on," she muttered.

"Huh?" Grant looked up from squirting ketchup on his fries.

Zara shrugged. "Nothing. Just trying to figure out what Fitz sees in Kate."

"What's not to like?" Grant glanced over toward the other couple. "She's gorgeous, and seems sweet. At least I know Tommi really likes her."

"Gorgeous, huh?" Zara lifted an eyebrow. "No wonder you wanted them to sit with us. Hoping she'd press up against you in the booth?"

"Stop." He looked uncomfortable. "I so didn't mean it like that, and you know it. It's no secret I think you're the hottest thing going, so don't get all weird about this, okay?"

"You sure about that?" Zara shot another look at the other couple. "If you're into the bony, boyish look, Kate's your girl. She's got about as many curves as a yardstick."

"Be nice," Grant said, looking even more uncomfortable.

Whatever. Zara decided it was time to take control of this whole boring conversation. Get Grant's attention back where it belonged.

She kicked off her sandal and started running her bare toes up his leg, then inside the hem of his khaki shorts. He gulped, put his fork down, and looked at her. She grinned.

"What do you say we get out of here?" she suggested. "We can get a doggie bag for the burgers."

He nodded, his face looking red again, then glanced around for their waitress. "Check, please!" he called.

FOURTEEN

The next few days passed quickly for Tommi. Almost before she knew it, it was Thursday afternoon. This weekend's show was a big, busy, popular one in the northern part of Zone 2. A lot of barns came down for it from Zone 1, which meant there were a lot of people and horses there that Tommi mostly only saw at the big winter shows in Florida.

But she wasn't focused on socializing this time. She had at least two much more important things on her mind. Legs and Alex.

She was lungeing Legs in a deserted schooling ring, getting him ready for tomorrow's jumper class, when she felt her phone vibrate in her pocket. Pulling it out, she saw it was another text from Alex: *Miss u! Wish your show wasn't so far away.*

Smiling, she quickly texted back: *Me too. But I'll see u when I get home.*

She hit Send, then glanced at Legs. He was trotting around steadily, looking sound and fit and ready to go. Good. Maybe all the schooling rides she'd put on him the last few days at home had paid off. Best of all, there was no sign of whatever it was she'd felt the other week. She was starting to wonder if she'd imagined the whole thing. Normally she wasn't the type to borrow trouble like that, but whatever. Maybe it was time to put that particular stress behind her.

The phone buzzed again in her hand. *Would rather see u right now; too bored w/o u.*

Sweet. Alex's parents were still away, so he'd crashed with a friend in the city over the weekend, and he and Tommi had gotten together every night until she left, hitting a few music clubs, going dancing, and just hanging out. They'd had so much fun she'd almost hated to leave town again for this show. Almost. She was really looking forward to proving to herself that Legs was just fine.

"Canter," she told the horse, adding a cluck and a little swish of the tail end of the line to encourage him. Not that Legs ever needed much encouragement to speed up. He broke into a canter immediately, building speed quickly.

Tommi got him slowed down to a more reasonable pace, then started composing another one-handed response to Alex, spinning on her heel as the horse circled around her. Just then she heard someone call her name.

Glancing up, she saw a girl around her own age standing at the rail. She was dressed in fringed custom chaps over breeches and a Joules polo, and for a second Tommi didn't recognize her. But then it clicked.

"Hey, Vanessa," she called. "What's up?"

She returned her attention to Legs, expecting the girl to

move on. After all, it wasn't as if they were friends—not even horse-show friends, really. Vanessa was the daughter of some big-time real estate developer in Boston. She rode at one of the nicer barns up there, where she kept a string of winning jumpers. Rarely the same ones from one year to the next, though. She tended to use them up fast by always wanting to jump more, jump higher, jump jump jump. She was an aggressive rider and won a lot, but had a rep for not being quite as talented as she thought she was.

When Tommi brought Legs to a halt and unhooked the lunge line a few minutes later, she was surprised to see Vanessa still standing there. "Cute horse," Vanessa called. "Yours?"

"Uh-huh. Sale project," Tommi said. "So your barn decided to come out for this one, huh?"

"Yeah, and I'm glad we did." Vanessa smoothed her glossy dark hair with one hand. "I already won my first division, not that anyone was surprised. I mean, at the last show I was one-two in the High Juniors, and then my green horse and I just barely missed reserve champion in his first division, and . . ."

There was more, but Tommi only pretended to listen as she clipped a lead to her horse's halter, folded up the lunge line, and got ready to go. Now she remembered the other reason Vanessa wasn't one of her favorite people. The girl was full of herself and seriously obnoxious.

"Congrats," Tommi said the first chance she had to get a word in edgewise. "Listen, I'd better get this guy back to the barn. See you around."

"Don't you ever sit still?" Dani said. "It makes me tired just watching you."

Kate tightened the girth of the big flea-bitten gray gelding she was tacking up in the cross-ties. Then she glanced at the other girl, who was perched on an overturned bucket in the aisle, fiddling with the laces of her field boots.

"Jamie decided to scratch that new Dutch horse from the Level Threes, so he offered to give Mrs. Walsh a quick extra lesson now that he has a little spare time. Miguel's still out picking up more shavings and I'm not sure what happened to Javier, so I said I could tack up Moonie before I have to start lungeing those ponies." Kate patted the gray gelding, who had one hind leg cocked lazily. He barely flicked an ear as she did up the girth one more hole. "Anyway, you know how it is at shows," she went on. "There's always way too much to do."

"Yeah, but you're the same way at home." Dani grinned. "I swear, you could run the whole freaking barn all by yourself."

Just then Mrs. Walsh hurried up to them. She was one of the wealthiest clients in the barn, but that wasn't why everyone from the grooms to the pony riders to the other adults liked her. She always had a smile and a kind word for everyone, and frequently turned up at shows bearing cookies or cupcakes that she'd baked herself. So maybe she wasn't the best baker in the world, but somehow nobody minded. It was still better than most horse-show food.

"Thank you so much, Kate," Mrs. Walsh said, her cheeks dimpling with pleasure as she gazed at her horse. "He looks wonderful." At the sound of her voice, the gray gelding immediately woke up and stretched his neck toward his owner, nuzzling her for treats. She pulled a peppermint out of the pocket of her high-waisted Pikeur breeches and fed it to him. "Jamie is meeting me at that little ring behind the tack vendor."

"I'll bring him up as soon as I get his bridle on, Mrs. Walsh," Kate promised.

"Wonderful." Mrs. Walsh beamed at her. "By the way, I've been meaning to ask you—I've been having a spot of trouble with my mare lately. You know me and my silly nerves." She laughed ruefully and shook her head. "In any case, I've decided I'm not up for showing her this time. It seems a shame to bring her all the way up here just to sit in her stall. Would you have any interest in showing her in the Junior Hunters on Saturday?"

Normally Kate would have jumped at the chance to show Mrs. Walsh's mare, a fabulously keen and impeccably trained Selle Français with an amazing jump. Today, though, she hesitated.

"Um, that's really nice of you to offer," she said. "But I don't think I can. I already told Jamie I'd ride two of his in the Schooling Hunters, and I think it might run at the same time."

"Oh, dear. What bad luck." Mrs. Walsh shrugged. "I suppose I'll see if Tommi has time for one more, then."

"I'll mention it to her for you if I see her first," Kate promised, already feeling guilty.

As soon as the woman left to find her helmet, Dani stared at Kate. "Are you nuts?" she said. "That horse is amazing! I'm sure Jamie wouldn't mind shuffling the order so you could do her in the Juniors."

Kate shrugged. "I know. But like you were just saying, I'm

pretty busy," she mumbled. "I've already got those two in the Schoolings, then the eq is right after that, plus a bunch more hunter stuff on Sunday. Oh, and the first one in the Schoolings is that cute little chestnut greenie who takes forever to warm up."

A nervous shiver ran through her when she mentioned the chestnut horse—her first show-ring trip of the week. Not that she was worried about the ride itself. The chestnut gelding was a sweetheart who tried his heart out every time, even if he didn't quite know what he was doing yet.

No, it was the showing part that was the problem. Specifically, the fact that when she'd arrived a couple of days ago, Kate had realized that her show clothes weren't fitting very well. Somehow it seemed she'd lost a bunch of weight over the past couple of weeks without even noticing, to the point that she'd gone down a full size if not two.

She was pretty sure she could get away with the show shirt if she pinned it, and her jacket was dark and structured enough that it didn't look too bad—plus she only had to slip that on long enough for the actual classes, where nobody would see her up close. Her boots were feeling a little looser than usual, but they would do, too.

The big problem was her breeches. Even at a distance, it was impossible to miss how baggy they were. They were a knock-off of Tailored Sportsmans side-zips, made with the same type of minimal-stretch fabric, which meant they really didn't conform to her body much at all. If she didn't cinch them with a belt, they'd slip right down past her hipbones. And they were her only decent pair.

It was lucky that Jamie hadn't asked her to ride anything

earlier in the week. After the way he'd gotten after her for not eating and sleeping enough or whatever it was that time, she definitely didn't want him to notice she'd lost so much weight. He'd probably get the wrong idea, maybe force her to cut back on working and riding. And she definitely didn't want that.

As long as she wasn't actually showing, she'd been able to manage. She'd been wearing jeans while she worked, though even those were so loose that she'd put on a pair of leggings underneath despite the heat. But she couldn't ignore the problem any longer, not with less than thirty-six hours until that first class.

"Well, your loss is Tommi's gain, I guess," Dani said, still looking dubious.

"Yeah, I guess." Kate quickly slipped the bit into the gray's mouth, then did up the noseband and throatlatch. "I'd better get Moonie up to the ring. See you."

"Sure you don't want to pop an Advil and come along?" Dani checked her makeup in the hotel room mirror, then grabbed her purse. She looked adorable in a V-neck cami and tight denim shorts, her henna-red hair swept back in a perky ponytail. Probably hoping some cute local guys might be hanging around the restaurant trolling for horse-show girls, Kate figured.

"Thanks, but I think my head'll feel better if I just get some sleep. I'm not that hungry anyway." Kate adjusted the pillow behind her head.

"Okay. I'll try to remember to bring you something back in case you feel like eating later."

"Thanks." Kate waited until the other girl pulled the door of their shared hotel room shut behind her. Then she hopped to her feet and hurried over to her suitcase. She was running out of time to deal with her clothing emergency. This could be her best chance.

Pulling out her show breeches, she tossed them on the bed. Then she dug into her cosmetics bag for the little sewing kit that she always carried in there but hardly ever used. Actually, she wasn't sure she'd ever touched it aside from the little card of safety pins. But when she found it, she saw that it had what she needed—needles and thread, a seam ripper, even a tiny pair of scissors.

She grabbed it, flopped down on the bed with the breeches, then froze, wishing she'd paid more attention in home ec. Sure, she'd repaired the occasional hem on her clothes or patched a saddle pad. But nothing this elaborate. Could she really do this?

"Nat," she whispered, suddenly realizing exactly where to turn for advice. Natalie loved clothes, and didn't have much more money to spend on them than Kate did. She was always ripping up anything that was too small or out of style and turning it into something else. Even claimed off and on that she wanted to be a fashion designer when she grew up. Some of her experiments turned out better than others, but at least she had the basics of sewing down pretty well. She'd know what to do if anyone would.

"What's up, Katie?" Nat said when she answered Kate's call. "You at your show or whatever?"

"Yeah." Kate was glad that Natalie seemed to be in a good

mood. The two of them hadn't spoken since last weekend's Happy Acres show, but they'd texted back and forth a couple of times.

"Too bad—hot party tonight at Jackie's. Just waiting for my ride now. But hey, what do you need parties for these days? Speaking of which, how's that cute rich boyfriend of yours?"

Well, at least Fitz had been upgraded from just "rich" to cute *and* rich. Kate guessed that meant Nat had been impressed.

"Um, fine," she said. "But listen, I need some sewing advice."

"Some what?"

"I'm here at this show, and I need to, like, adjust the seam of my breeches," Kate said, not wanting to get into too many details. "And it has to look good—they're kind of picky about that sort of thing here, and—"

"Yeah, I know." Kate could almost hear Nat rolling her eyes over the phone. "Those rich snobs are all about looking good, right?"

Kate bit her lip, letting that pass. "Anyway, you're the best sewer I know. So what do I need to do to take these in without ruining them?"

"Ask Fitz to get one of his servants to do it?" Natalie laughed. "Seriously, Katie. That boy is smitten. It was totally obvious from the second I saw you two together."

For once, Kate didn't mind her teasing. At least not too much. It showed that they were back—BFFs again. Making the effort to go to that schooling show had been worth it. Even if she'd had to bite her tongue the whole time about that poor confused Thoroughbred Nat was "training."

"Okay, but what's plan B?" she asked. "I've got the seam

ripper and some scissors, but I'm sitting here panicking in case I take everything apart and can't get it back together."

"Chill, it's not brain surgery," Nat said. "Just use the seam ripper to slice through the threads. Usually you can pull it apart after a few rips to make it go faster."

"Then?"

"Duh. Then you sew it all back together again. Just line it up the way you want it, maybe pin it if you can." There was a loud buzz in the background. "Oops! Dan's here to pick me up. Gotta go. Good luck with the breeches!"

"Wait!" Kate cried.

Too late. Nat had already hung up.

Kate set down her phone and stared at the breeches lying in front of her, trying to psych herself up. Okay, that hadn't been much help. But like Nat said, it wasn't brain surgery. She could do this.

"Here goes nothing," she whispered, grabbing the breeches.

Her hand shook as she picked up the seam ripper. That made it even harder to get the little pointy part under the tight stitches of the side seam. Kate forced herself to stop and take a deep breath, then try again. This time she managed to rip out one stitch. Then another. The third stitch seemed even tinier and tighter, so she wriggled the seam ripper to try to wedge it in there.

RRRRRRIP!

Kate gasped as her hand slipped, shoving the seam ripper past the thread. "No!" she cried, not wanting to look but unable to turn away. She'd just sliced a big gash in the fabric itself.

She tossed aside the seam ripper and poked at the spot.

Maybe it was only one layer, maybe it wasn't as bad as she thought.

But it was. If anything, it was worse. As if her too-big breeches hadn't been bad enough, now there was a big rip right on the butt, below where the hem of her coat would fall. No way would Jamie let her anywhere near the ring like that!

She glanced at the phone again, tempted to call Nat back. But no. She couldn't help her now—nobody could. With a sick, helpless feeling in the pit of her stomach, Kate picked up the seam ripper again.

By the time she heard Dani's footsteps in the hallway two hours later, Kate was almost in tears. She'd finished ripping out the seam, hoping that by the time she took it in, the rip wouldn't show.

But it did. Plus the new seam she'd tried to sew looked horrible, amateurish and sloppy. She wished she'd just left the breeches the way they were, maybe tried wearing them over her pajama bottoms or something to make them fit better. But it was too late now. Way too late.

She barely had time to hide the ruined breeches, jump into bed, and pretend to be sleeping before Dani came in. An hour later Dani had showered, changed, and fallen asleep herself, but Kate was still lying there wide awake, wondering exactly what in the world she was supposed to do now.

FIFTEEN

——— ——— ——— ——— ———

"Nicely done," Jamie said as Zara rode out of the ring.

Zara grinned. She didn't need anyone to tell her that she and Keeper had just burned up that junior jumper class. Still, it was good to hear. Jamie wasn't exactly loose with the compliments.

"Thanks," she said, giving Keeper a pat. "That was fun."

She rode past the gate congestion, then swung down and loosened the horse's girth. Max hurried toward her.

"I'll cool him out for you if you want to watch your friends go," the young groom offered.

Zara glanced over her shoulder and saw Tommi riding Legs into the ring. "Great, thanks," she said, handing Max the reins. "Think I will."

Her friends, huh? So at least one person thought she was fitting in at her new barn. Was she? Zara still wasn't sure, but she wasn't in the mood for philosophizing about it just then.

She hurried back and found a spot at the rail just as Tommi

picked up the canter. Legs looked good. Sharp. His ears were at full alert, flicking back and forth from Tommi to the coming fence.

"Chill, dude," Zara whispered as Legs spurted forward, almost running past his distance. Tommi steadied him, meeting the fence just right and sailing over with inches to spare.

"Do you know that horse?" someone asked from beside Zara.

It was a fish-faced girl with shiny dark hair. Full makeup, pricey custom chaps, a bracelet that looked like real diamonds.

"You talking to me?" Zara asked, half expecting her to start gushing about how much she loved Zac's music.

But the girl was already looking back at the ring. Zara wasn't even sure she'd actually recognized her. "I'm Vanessa," she said. "I heard that horse Tommi Aaronson is riding might be for sale. True?"

"Yeah, actually he is." Zara turned to watch as the pair approached another jump. "Why, you interested?"

"Maybe." Vanessa watched closely as Legs landed, then made a sharp turn to a big, airy vertical. "Wanted to see him go first. I don't waste my time with average jumpers. Anything I ride has to have serious talent."

Zara didn't have time to roll her eyes. She held her breath as Legs neared the vertical. It was a tricky one, and it came up really fast after that last jump. Even Keeper had given the thing a hard look, and he was as been-there-done-that as could be in the jumper ring.

Sure enough, Legs raised his head and slowed down a bit. But Tommi was ready, keeping him balanced and in front of her leg while tactfully pushing him forward. He took off a hair long but had no trouble clearing it.

"Nice," Zara murmured. It was pretty obvious that Tommi wasn't riding for the time or a ribbon. She was taking it easy, finessing the course, making sure Legs felt confident and had a good experience. Smart.

"He looks pretty scopey, huh? You seen him school much at home? Is he usually a little faster? I almost always make the jump-off, so I need a fast horse."

Zara had almost forgotten about Vanessa already. She glanced over. "Well, I don't usually waste my time watching other people's horses," she said with a straight face. "But yeah, I've seen him go a lot."

"And?"

Was this girl for real? Zara was starting to get annoyed by her attitude. As if the whole world was her own personal Google, and other people existed solely for the purpose of telling her what she needed to know.

But after her own good ride, Zara was in too good a mood to tell her off. Besides, why bother when messing with her was so much more fun?

"And he's probably the most talented jumper I've ever seen," she said, putting as much sincerity into her voice and face as she could. Gina wasn't the only one in the family who could act. "Seriously. Jamie can't believe he's lucky enough to have this horse in his barn."

"You mean Jamie Vos? He said that?" The girl actually looked impressed. "Really?"

"Would I lie to you?" Zara fought to keep her smile from

turning into a smirk. "Anyway, Tommi's being superconservative with him—that's the only reason she's bothering with even schooling him in the piddly old juniors." She glanced around, as if making sure nobody was eavesdropping. "If you ask me, they'll probably be doing a lot more by the time they get to indoors. A *lot*." She raised her eyebrows, then shot a not-so-subtle glance in the direction of the Grand Prix ring just across the way.

"Interesting." Vanessa watched as Tommi guided Legs over the final jump on the course, then eased him to a trot and rode toward the gate.

Zara didn't answer. For one thing, she was already getting bored with this girl. Besides, she'd just noticed that Dani's horse was acting up as she tried to ride him through the mess around the gate. Some woman was letting her corgi dash back and forth on his flexi leash, and it was making the always-amped Thoroughbred nervous. Jamie and Miguel saw it, too, and were already hurrying over to help. Glancing around, Zara saw that none of the other grooms were in view. That meant Tommi was on her own. Sure, she could probably handle it. But why not help out if she could?

"Gotta go," she told Vanessa.

She hurried over to meet Tommi as she came out of the ring. "Thanks," Tommi said as Zara took Legs's reins and guided him through the chaos to a quieter spot. "How'd we look?"

"Great." Zara grinned. "And hey, if I help you sell Legs, do I get a commission?"

Tommi dismounted and unhooked her helmet strap. "What are you talking about?"

"Just kidding around. This chick at the rail was asking me all kinds of questions about him being for sale and stuff. Guess she's kind of interested. So I talked him up a little."

"Really? Who was it?" Tommi craned her head to look back at the ring.

Zara glanced over at where the girl had been standing, but there was no sign of her. "Looks like she took off. Oh well, guess you'll find out if she actually gets in touch."

"Yeah." Tommi sounded a little distracted. She smiled as she gave Legs a pat, then fished a treat out of her pocket. "Guess so."

"Aha! There you are!" Fitz suddenly appeared in the doorway of the feed stall, where Kate was measuring out dry beet pulp shreds. Dinnertime was still several hours away, but more than half of the horses were showing or schooling at the moment, and she wanted to take advantage of the relative quiet.

Fitz swooped in, grabbed her by the hand, and pulled her after him into the aisle. "What are you doing?" Kate protested. "I'm right in the middle of something."

"I don't care." He grinned at her. "Jamie just finished telling me how much I suck in pretty much every possible way, and I'm feeling vulnerable and insecure. I need a Kate fix to give me a reason to go on living."

Yeah, right. Jamie might be angry with Fitz right now, but that wouldn't affect his professional, positive training style. And *vulnerable* and *insecure* weren't the first two words anyone would ever use to describe Fitz. They weren't even on the list.

Still, Kate couldn't resist following along as he led her down the aisle. For one thing, she knew it would be faster to give in than to argue about it. Besides, she could use a little mental break herself. It had been another crazy-busy day so far, and it didn't help that she still had no idea what to do about her ruined breeches. She'd peeked at them again that morning, hanging back after Dani left for breakfast, and they looked even worse in the cold gray light of dawn.

That was a real problem. It wasn't as if she could ride tomorrow's Big Eq class in jeans. Or even in her schooling breeches, a cheap pair of tan Tuff Rider pull-ons that were old and a little faded but relatively clean. They would've fit right in at that Happy Acres show, but they wouldn't fly here. If worse came to worst, she figured she'd have to fake an attack of food poisoning or something to get out of showing entirely. But the thought of doing something like that made her feel sick for real. Jamie had brought Fable to this show mostly for her, and she hated to let him down. Not to mention that he'd have to scramble to find someone else to ride those greenies in the schooling division or else rearrange everyone's schedule and run himself ragged adding them to his own overcrowded list.

She forgot about all that as Fitz pulled her into an unoccupied stall. "That's more like it," he murmured as he took her gently by the shoulders and planted a soft kiss on her lips. "Maybe I *can* find the strength to go on after all."

Despite her worries, Kate smiled. She didn't know how Fitz did it. He had such a goofy, relaxed, lighthearted way of looking at things, and it rubbed off on everyone around him. Even her.

"Are you sure?" she said, leaning into him. "You still look kind of depressed to me."

Fitz laughed. "Come to think of it, better safe than sorry."

He bent toward her for another kiss. As things quickly got more intense, his hands slid from her shoulders around to her back, then down to her waist. He gave her a little squeeze, then pulled back. There was a slight frown on his face.

"Hey," he said, running his hands up and down her sides again, pausing at the ribs and hipbones. "Are you okay? You'd tell me if you were sick or something, right?"

Kate pulled back, pushing his hands away. "What are you talking about? I'm fine." She tugged at the baggy polo shirt she was wearing over a thick ribbed T-shirt.

"Hello?" a voice called in the aisle outside. "Anybody here?"

"That's Tommi." Kate turned away, ignoring the concern in Fitz's hazel eyes. "Better go see what she needs."

Tommi was in the aisle, leading Legs. "Oh!" Kate said, realizing she'd forgotten to run out to watch her friend's jumper round. "How'd it go?"

"Fine. Slow but clear, which is what I was aiming for." Tommi pointed at Fitz. "Jamie's looking for you. And he's not in a patient mood right now, if you know what I mean."

Fitz grimaced. "Unfortunately, I do." He shot Kate one last look, then bent to plant a light kiss on her forehead. "See you, gorgeous."

When he'd gone, Kate turned and found Tommi staring at her. "You okay?" Tommi asked. "You look kind of upset. Fitz isn't pushing you too hard again, is he?"

"No, no, it's nothing like that," Kate said quickly. Tommi was the only one who knew about that night in the hay stall. "Fitz is great. It's just that I really shouldn't be wasting any time hanging out with him right now. I've got way too much to do." Realizing it was true, she hurried off before Tommi could say another word.

SIXTEEN

Tommi took her time getting Legs settled in his show stall, fussing over him and feeding him a few extra treats. She was proud of how he'd handled things in the ring today. He had his quirks, but he also had more heart and try than any horse she'd ridden in a long time.

She was still in the stall when she heard Miguel's voice out in the aisle. "I believe she's in with one of her horses, miss," the groom said. "Third one on that side."

Curious, Tommi stepped to the front of the stall and looked out. At first all she could see was Miguel leading a horse down the aisle. Then they passed her, and she saw Vanessa hurrying along after them.

"Tommi!" the girl said when she spotted her. "I was looking for you."

"You found me." Tommi ducked out under the stall guard. "What's up?"

Vanessa reached her, but she wasn't looking at Tommi. She

was staring past her at Legs, who'd come to the front of his stall to see what was going on.

"That's the horse, right? The one who's for sale?" Vanessa rubbed the gelding's face as he nosed at her curiously. "I just saw you take him in the High Juniors. Can he go any faster than that?"

Tommi frowned. "Of course," she said. "He's still green and is new to the Highs, so I'm giving him a chance to get used to the height and tight turns and stuff before we—"

"Okay, good, that's what I figured," Vanessa interrupted. "I'll want to see for myself, of course. But I'm thinking he could be the perfect ride to help me move up. My main horse now is maxed out, and I heard this guy has enough scope to do Grand Prix."

Grand Prix, huh? Remembering Zara's comment earlier, Tommi could guess where Vanessa had heard that. She tried to keep her expression neutral, though inwardly she was wincing. Gossip had it that Vanessa was already breaking down her current star, a really nice schoolmaster that her previous trainer had imported for her. He deserved better than that. And so did Legs.

She opened her mouth to tell the girl to forget it, that Legs wasn't for sale. Not to her.

But she could almost see her father's disapproving expression. *Listen, Thomasina, this isn't a game of My Little Pony. You're playing with real money here.*

Tommi wasn't the type to fret and second-guess herself, so she'd already moved on from her decision to scratch at the last show. At least she thought she had. Now she had to wonder, though—was she doing it again? Paying too much attention to her own worries and feelings, when this should really just be a straight business transaction?

"I don't know about Grand Prix, but Legs is a very talented jumper," she heard herself saying. "If you're serious about wanting to try him, bring your trainer by and we'll talk."

"Whoa, big guy," Kate said as Fable tossed his head and opened his stride, pulling her past their distance. She ducked to stay with him as he lurched over the vertical, then sat down to collect him on the other side. The second fence in their schooling line was only four strides away.

Make that three and a half strides. Fable ignored her aids, charging full steam ahead at the second obstacle and winding up too close again. He popped over with a grunt, pinning his ears as he landed.

"Ugh," Kate said aloud as she circled back around to the first jump. "Let's try that again."

Then she saw Jamie at the rail of the schooling ring, waving her down. It took a bit of an effort to turn Fable, who'd already locked onto the first fence again. Finally, though, she managed to slow him to a walk, then turned and rode back over to the trainer.

"Doing some schooling for tomorrow's eq?" Jamie asked.

Kate nodded, a little too breathless to speak for a second. "Yeah," she finally managed. "He's kind of full of himself today."

"I can see that." But Jamie wasn't looking at the horse. He was looking at Kate. "Look, I know you have a lot to do and probably aren't always thinking about what you're wearing," he said. "And you know I don't get too worked up about the dress code at home most of the time. But please keep in mind that when you're at a show, you're representing all of Pelham Lane's riders—and me—anytime you're on a horse."

Kate felt her cheeks go pink as she glanced down at herself. She was still dressed in jeans and that baggy polo. "Sorry, Jamie," she said. "Um, my show breeches got stained, and they're still at the hotel being dry-cleaned."

"I see." Jamie looked sympathetic. He knew all about Kate's financial status—after all, he was the one who'd given her a heads-up on those show breeches after spotting them in the consignment corner of a small tack shop in Connecticut. "Well, that's fine. But you can look tidy even when you're not in show clothes, right?"

This time Kate just nodded, not trusting herself to say a word. Sure, she'd thought about changing to her schooling breeches before she rode. But after remembering how even those had drooped off her when she'd tried them on that morning, she'd changed her mind and stuck with the jeans, even though they weren't particularly clean.

Fable was getting restless, slinging his head and trying to move off. Jamie glanced at the horse.

"Looked like Fable was pulling past your distances in that last line," he commented. "Next time, try doing some lateral work on your way to the fence. He used to be a dressage horse, remember—he knows how to do that. That'll make it harder for him to rush."

"Okay, thanks. I'll try that right now." Kate gathered her

reins. She'd caught her breath by then and was ready to get back to riding. Ready for this whole uncomfortable conversation to end.

"Good." Jamie checked his watch. "Oops, wish I could stay to watch. But I'm supposed to be meeting Tommi in the jumper schooling ring right now. Let me know how it goes, all right?"

"Okay."

Kate watched him go, feeling anxious. It was going to take more than a little dressage to fix her problems.

Usually the only time Tommi got nervous on a horse was when she was walking into the show ring. At those times, she always turned her nerves into adrenaline and determination, using it to make her performance better.

But she was having trouble doing that now, even though all she was doing was warming up Legs at the trot in a mostly empty schooling ring.

She glanced over to see if Vanessa had arrived yet. There was no sign of her or her trainer, or Jamie for that matter, though he'd promised to try to be there for moral support. However, Fitz and Dani were hanging out at the rail. Tommi had run into them while tacking up Legs, and they'd decided to tag along and watch.

"Good boy," Tommi told Legs, giving him a pat as she brought him back to a walk. That was enough of a warm-up. She didn't want to tire him out too much. He'd already had a pretty long day.

"He's looking good," Fitz called as Tommi walked the horse toward them.

"He feels good, especially considering he just finished showing like an hour and a half ago." Tommi stopped the horse by the rail. "Not that Vanessa let that stop her."

Dani snorted. "I know, right?" she said. "I feel sorry for her horses. She goes through them faster than you-know-who goes through girls." She shot Fitz a sly look.

"I have no idea who you're talking about," Fitz said with a smirk. "But you're so right about Vanessa. She uses them up fast, and dumps them even faster once they go lame or get sour or just stop winning."

"Or if she can't ride them and they make her look bad," Dani agreed. "I heard she got trashed all over the Internet last year when one of her old horses got rescued at some scuzzy auction all skinny and lame and on his way to kill."

"Seriously?" Fitz shook his head. "Wow, that's cold. It's not like her folks couldn't afford to retire every horse she's ever ridden."

Tommi felt more uneasy than ever as she listened to them. "Hold on, you guys. Are you sure she's still like that?" she put in. "She switched trainers last winter, remember? Her new one's got a good rep—Abby Durand-Evans. Maybe she's shown Vanessa the error of her ways."

"Maybe." Fitz didn't sound too convinced. Dani just shrugged.

They all stopped talking about it as Jamie arrived. "Legs ready to go?" he asked Tommi, checking his watch. "Abby just texted me—they're on their way."

Tommi nodded, relieved to see him. Yeah, this was supposed to be her project. But it was nice to have him there backing her up.

"He might be a little tired from that class earlier," she told Jamie. "But I think he'll do fine."

"Good." Jamie was peering across the ring at the path on the opposite side. "Here they come."

Vanessa's trainer was a short, brisk woman with thick blond hair pulled back in a ponytail. She shook hands with Tommi and introduced herself.

"I caught part of your warm-up before your class earlier," she said. "He looks like an overachiever."

Tommi chuckled. "That's a good word for it," she said. "He takes some finesse, but he'll try his heart out if he understands what you want from him." She glanced at Vanessa, who was buckling on her helmet, then back to the trainer. "Do you want to see some flatwork first, or should I just go ahead and jump a line or something?"

"Forget that," Vanessa said before her trainer could speak. "I already saw you ride him in the show ring before. I'm ready to take him for a spin myself."

Tommi hesitated. "Um, okay," she said when neither Jamie nor Abby protested. She slid down. "You okay riding in my saddle?"

"Sure, whatever." Vanessa ducked between the fence rails into the ring, then stepped over to adjust the stirrup length. Legs twisted his neck around to nose at her, but she pushed his head away. "Give me a leg up," she ordered.

Tommi thought she was talking to her until she saw that

— 192 —

Abby had ducked into the ring, too. "Could you hold him, please?" the trainer asked Tommi. Then she turned to help Vanessa into the saddle.

"He likes a light hand and a steady leg," Tommi said as she released her grip on the reins. Vanessa didn't say anything, though Abby smiled and thanked Tommi.

For the next few minutes, Tommi stood with Jamie and the others and watched as Vanessa's trainer guided her through about five minutes of flatwork, then started jumping. They began by going back and forth over the three-foot line Tommi had used to warm up. Then Vanessa wanted to try something higher, so Abby set the vertical to 3'6" and the back rail of the oxer a little higher.

"Come in nice and easy," the trainer called.

Vanessa nodded, then kicked Legs into a brisk canter. The horse pricked his ears at the jump, and Tommi could see him hesitate. Her body tensed with the aids she would have given—a slight half-halt to balance him, coupled with more leg to send him forward.

"Git up!" Vanessa growled loudly, turning her foot out and jabbing the horse with both spurs.

Legs's head shot up, and he spurted forward. Tommi winced as he flung himself over the jump and galloped toward the next one.

"At least that proves he's honest," Fitz murmured in Tommi's ear as the horse flew over the oxer.

"Bring him around and try it again," Abby called. "A little less leg this time."

Things continued pretty much the same way for a while.

They jumped the new line several times, then raised the jumps again. And again after that. The horse's hooves never even came close to touching a rail despite a few scary distances. But Tommi could see him starting to get frazzled.

"Put it up again," Vanessa called to her trainer as she landed from the oxer yet again. "Let's see how high he can go."

Tommi bit her lip. They were already at the maximum height Tommi had schooled with Legs so far. And now Vanessa wanted to go higher? No way. It was time to put a stop to this before Legs totally freaked out.

She shot a look at Jamie, hoping—and half expecting—that he might do it for her. But he was leaning on the rail nearby, watching with a neutral expression as Abby stepped over to set the fence.

That made Tommi hesitate. If two experienced trainers didn't see a problem with this, who was she to second-guess them? Maybe this was normal for the trial of a high-level jumper. Maybe Legs was handling it better than she thought.

Before she could decide, Vanessa was bringing him around again. He wobbled a bit on the approach, acting as if he might be thinking about running out. But Vanessa held him on the track and he ended up going over. He gave the vertical a hard rub with one hind leg, but cleared the oxer with room to spare. Vanessa didn't even slow down, taking him around again, and this time he sailed over both.

"You were right, this horse can jump," Vanessa called to Tommi as she hauled the horse to a stop. Legs jigged, looking sweaty and a bit wild-eyed, but the girl didn't seem to notice. She glanced at her trainer. "He'll be perfect for me, don't you think?"

"You look good on him," Abby replied.

Vanessa nodded, looking pleased. "I'll have to clear it with my parents first, of course," she told Tommi. "But I'm sure we'll be in touch soon."

Tommi felt vaguely queasy as she untacked Legs back at the stabling tent. She was just pulling the saddle off the horse's back when Zara wandered by with Chaucer at her heels.

"How'd it go?" Zara asked. "I heard someone just tried him. Was it that girl I talked to earlier? I forget her name—Veronica or something, maybe?"

"Vanessa. Yeah, it was her. And Legs was a good boy," Tommi said as she bent to unhook his boots. "Actually, that's an understatement."

"What do you mean?" Zara dug into her breeches pocket and came up with a horse treat for Legs. "They got along really well?"

"Not exactly." Tommi grimaced as she remembered some of the highlights. She felt pretty certain that Legs wouldn't tolerate Vanessa's impatient, ham-handed riding for long if she ended up buying him. He was likely to end up just like the rest of her rejects, dumped and forgotten.

She gave Zara the CliffsNotes version of the trial ride. "Wow," Zara said when she finished. "So are you actually going to sell him to her, or what?"

"I don't know." Tommi grabbed a brush out of her grooming tote. "I mean, I really like this horse and he has a ton of talent. I'd rather wait and find someone better for him—a rider who can bring him to his full potential and still treat him well, you know?"

"Sure. So you tell this wench no sale, life goes on." Zara shrugged. "Easy."

"Not exactly." Tommi started brushing the saddle marks out of Legs's glossy bay coat. "It's kind of tempting to just go for it. Get him off the books ASAP. That's sure to impress my dad—he's all about the quick close." She smiled wryly. "And Vanessa's kind of famous for paying too much for all her horses. I doubt she'll even try to haggle on my asking price."

"Okay." Zara bent to play with Chaucer's ears. "So sell, then. What's the worst that could happen?"

"Probably not much," Tommi said. "I mean, I'm sure it wouldn't be long before Legs bucked her off one too many times. She's likely to get sick of him way before she has a chance to break him down, and her trainer'll snap him up for somebody else in her barn. Or at least convince her to sell him on to a decent show home."

"Cool. Then it's a win-win," Zara said. "Right?"

Tommi ran her brush over the tired horse, who was trying to stretch the cross-ties enough to reach out and nose at the dog.

"Right," Tommi said, trying hard to convince herself that it was true.

SEVENTEEN

Saturday morning came early, just like every other show day.
But Kate woke up even before the alarm went off, staring up
at the hotel room ceiling and listening to Dani snore and mut-
ter in the next bed. This was it. She was supposed to show
several horses today, including Fable in the eq. And she had
yet to figure out what to do about her breeches situation.

She was still lying there when the buzzer sounded. Dani
didn't move for a long moment, then finally stirred, pushed
herself up into a sitting position, and smacked at the alarm
until it shut off.

"Ugh," she moaned, shoving a chunk of hair out of her face.
"Remind me again why we do this?"

Kate sat up, too. "I don't know," she said, too distracted to
play along.

Dani swung her legs over the side of her bed. "First dibs
on the shower," she muttered sleepily.

She disappeared into the bathroom. Kate just sat there,

her mind skittering around as frantically as a weanling newly separated from its mother. She knew she should just ask one of her friends to loan her a pair of breeches. It was the only possible way she'd still be able to ride today. Even Dani, whose family had to budget carefully to afford her riding, usually had a spare pair of Tailored Sportsmans on hand in case of stains or other disasters.

The trouble was, Dani was an athlete and built like one. She was also several inches shorter than Kate. Glancing toward the bathroom door, behind which she could hear Dani humming over the sound of the shower, Kate knew there was no way her breeches would come close to fitting well enough to pass. Especially now.

Kate ran through the other options in her mind. Marissa was almost as tall as she was, but nowhere near as slim. Tommi was slim, but quite a bit shorter. What about Zara? She was a lot curvier than Kate and not so tall, but tended to favor form-fitting styles. Kate might be able to make something of hers work. But anytime she thought about asking her, her stomach clenched and she kind of wanted to cry. When it came right down to it, she hated the idea of asking any of her wealthier friends for anything. It just wasn't her.

"It's not that big a deal," she murmured aloud, trying to convince herself.

She stood up and dug into her suitcase, pulling out the ripped breeches. If she showed them to her friends, maybe came up with a good story to explain what had happened, she knew any of them would immediately offer to help. Probably even loan her enough cash to pick up a new pair in her size at the tack vendors.

That reminded Kate of those pricey show gloves Zara had bought her, which were laid out on the dresser along with her helmet and crop. She still felt guilty for accepting those. Hadn't even really wanted to wear them today, though she'd just about convinced herself that Zara might be insulted if she didn't. How could she accept even more from her—from any of them?

As she stared at the gloves, a new idea popped into her head. Kind of a crazy one. Crazy enough to work? Kate squeezed the gloves in her hand, not sure she'd have the guts to try it.

Then again, what other choice did she have?

Kate glanced up from picking out a horse's foot when she heard footsteps coming her way. But it was only Zara. She was munching on a doughnut, probably swiped from the hotel's breakfast buffet.

"Hey," she said. "You showing today?"

Kate's stomach grumbled as she watched the other girl take another bite. She'd been so busy watching for Summer at breakfast that she'd barely eaten a thing.

But this was no time to think about food. "Um, yeah," she told Zara. "I'm doing two of Jamie's in the schoolings in a couple of hours, then Fable right after that."

"Cool. Light day today for me." Zara leaned against the wall and picked at her cuticles. "I should probably get a new eq horse myself—give me something to do." She glanced up and grinned. "Besides, my father owes me."

Kate had no idea what she was talking about. But she was starting to feel nervous. Zara couldn't be here if she was going to put her plan into action. She had to get rid of her. But how? Zara wasn't the type to volunteer to run to the office to pick up numbers or anything like that.

"Um, hey," she said as an idea popped into her head. "I heard some girls from another barn gossiping about some super cute guy riding in one of the schooling rings right now. Did you see him?"

"Really? No," Zara said, suddenly perking up. "Seriously, a real live hottie at a horse show? Is he straight?"

"I don't know, they didn't say. It sounded like it, though."

Zara grinned. "Thanks for the tip; I think I just found something to do. Want to come check it out with me?"

"I wish." Kate gestured with her hoof pick at the horse in the cross-ties. "Can't. Sorry."

"Your loss." Zara hurried out without a backward glance.

Kate breathed a sigh of relief, fighting back a few pangs of guilt. Okay, now all she had to do was find Summer. She hadn't made it to breakfast before Kate had to leave, so it was now or never. Kate put the horse back in its stall and started to search.

Ten minutes later, she tracked her down in the tack stall. Summer was sitting on one of the director's chairs watching her dog, Whiskey, jump around and nip at Chaucer, who was trying to sleep.

"Hi," Kate said, glancing around to make sure nobody else was nearby. All clear.

Summer shot her an uninterested look. "Hi." Then she went back to watching the dogs.

Her hands shaking, Kate pulled the Roeckl gloves out of

her jeans pocket. "Hey," she said, trying to sound casual. "Check out my new show gloves. Do you like them?"

"They're okay, I guess." Summer barely glanced at the gloves.

"Yeah, Zara must think so, too," Kate said. "She has the exact same pair."

"Really?" For the first time, Summer's pale blue eyes showed a glimmer of interest. "Are you sure they're the same?"

"Absolutely. I was with her when she bought them." Kate flapped the gloves against her other palm. "She's been wearing them this whole show, didn't you notice?"

"Well, of course I noticed she looked amazing, as usual." Summer hopped to her feet, hurried over, and plucked the gloves out of Kate's hand. She pulled one on, then held her hand out to admire it. "I should probably get a pair of these myself. I wonder if they sell them at the tack vendor here?"

"I don't think so." Kate shrugged, still working hard to keep it casual. "But if you really like them, I guess you could buy these off of me. I don't really need them, and they're brand-new—I haven't even worn them yet."

"Seriously? It's a deal!" Summer clutched the gloves to herself, as if fearing Kate might change her mind and grab them back. "I'll pay you back for them later, okay?"

"No!" Kate blurted out, panicking. "Um, I mean if you want them, I kind of need the cash now. If you have it."

"Of course I have it." Summer rolled her eyes. "But I really don't feel like walking all the way out to the car to get it."

"I'll come with you." Kate kept her voice firm. "We can go right now."

Summer hesitated, glancing down at the gloves. Then she sighed. "Fine," she said. "Let's go."

Kate led the way out of the tack stall, knowing she'd feel better once Summer's money was in her pocket. True, fifty bucks still wasn't enough to buy her a new pair of name-brand breeches at the tack vendors. But if she pooled it with the cash she had left from her food budget, she should be able to swing something acceptable.

As they rounded the corner at the end of the aisle, Kate felt her heart stop. Zara was coming the other way. She was staring down at her cell phone with a self-satisfied smile.

"Wait, let's go back," Kate whispered, grabbing for Summer's arm.

But Summer was already rushing forward. "Zara!" she called excitedly, waving the gloves. "Check it out—we're going to match!"

Kate froze in place. This couldn't be happening. Somehow, she'd just assumed that Summer wouldn't tell anyone where she got those gloves. She was such a snob, she'd want everyone to think she'd bought them at some high-end tack store or something—not from the working student she looked down on.

But it seemed she'd been wrong. Zara was already glancing up, looking confused and a little annoyed. All Kate could do was brace herself for whatever was coming next.

Zara stared as Summer raced toward her. What the hell was the girl yapping about now, and why was she supposed to care?

She glanced down at the phone in her hand, more than a little distracted. She'd just hung up from talking to Grant. The boy was so hot for her it wasn't even funny.

Then she looked at Summer again. She was waving a pair of gloves in her face, sounding all excited.

Zara blinked as she realized those gloves looked familiar. She grabbed them out of Summer's hand.

"Hey," she said. "These are just like mine."

"That's what I'm telling you!" Summer gushed with that big, stupid smile of hers. "I figured if you liked them, they had to be awesome, right?"

Zara glanced at Kate. She was hanging back, looking like she wished she could disappear. Well, okay, she always kind of looked like that. But now more than ever.

Then Zara looked down at the gloves again. The ones just like hers. Just like the ones she'd bought for Kate.

"Listen, Zara," Kate began, her voice shaking a little. "I—"

"No, shut up," Zara cut in, finally catching on to what was happening here. "I don't want to hear it."

"But if you just let me explain," Kate said frantically. "I really didn't mean to—"

"I told you, I don't want to hear it!" Zara scowled at Kate, completely ignoring Summer, who was still buzzing around like the annoying little mosquito she was. But at least it had been obvious from the start that Summer was a loser user. On the other hand, Kate's big, pathetic puppy-dog eyes and soft voice had suckered her completely. And Zara hated being played for a chump.

"But—" Kate tried once more.

"But nothing," Zara snapped, waving the gloves in Kate's face. "Thanks for making me feel like a total dumbass, Kate. I thought we were friends, I tried to do something nice—guess I should've known better, huh? Believe me, I won't make that mistake again."

Spinning on her heel, she stuffed the gloves in her pocket and stomped away.

EIGHTEEN

Kate felt numb as she hurried down the aisle, looking for Jamie. It had been fifteen minutes since Zara had stormed off. That was how long it had taken Kate to realize that it was officially too late to fix things. Those gloves were gone, which meant there was no way she could come up with enough money for new breeches. So she had no choice. She had to tell Jamie the truth.

Well, most of the truth, anyway. She didn't have to tell him how the breeches got ruined. Just that she didn't have a suitable pair to wear in the show ring today. Maybe he'd take pity on her, loan her the money for a new pair and let her work it off somehow. Or maybe he'd just find someone else to ride those greenies and then take Fable in the eq. Either way, she wanted to allow him enough time to deal with what she'd done.

She stuck her head into the spare stall at the end of the row where the barn's feed and equipment were stored for the duration of the show. Miguel and Max were in there, the older groom sweeping up some spilled grain while Max scrubbed out a dirty bucket.

"Have you seen Jamie?" Kate asked the two grooms.

"Not lately," Max said. "Want me to text him for you?"

"Don't bother." Miguel glanced up from his work. "I just saw him talking to someone outside. If you hurry you might catch him there."

"Thanks." Kate headed out the barn's main entrance. Sure enough, Jamie was standing out there talking to a petite woman with a thick blond ponytail—Kate vaguely recognized her as another well-known trainer, though she couldn't recall the woman's name and was too distracted to try.

She hung back in the entryway, not wanting to interrupt the conversation. Jamie's back was to her, so he hadn't noticed her yet.

As she waited, she heard someone call her name. Glancing over her shoulder, she saw Mrs. Walsh hurrying toward her.

"Oh, dear!" the woman exclaimed. "I'm in such a state, Kate—I'm hoping you can be an angel and help me out."

"Sure, what is it?" Kate said automatically, even though one of Mrs. Walsh's mini-crises was the last thing she had time for right now.

"Just look at this!" Mrs. Walsh sort of fluttered her hands at herself. "Moonie just snotted all over my shirt, and it's the only clean one I have left! But I promised Greta I'd be there cheering her on in her adult equitation division, and Javier just left to take her horse to the warm-up ring."

Kate nodded, keeping one eye on Jamie. The trainer had just checked his watch. Uh-oh. That meant he was probably getting ready to dash over to the warm-up to meet Greta Phillips. If she didn't catch him now, Kate might miss her chance.

She opened her mouth to excuse herself. But Mrs. Walsh hadn't even paused for breath. "I know how busy you are, Kate, so I hate to ask," she was saying. "But is there any way you have time to run to the tack vendor's tent and pick me up a new shirt?"

Sorry, I can't, Kate wanted to tell her. Instead, she heard herself say, "Of course, no problem."

"Wonderful!" Mrs. Walsh beamed at her. "As long as you're over there, I suppose we'd better make it two shirts—I might add that extra hunter division tomorrow, and lord knows Moonie can never keep his slobber to himself." She chuckled and shook her head fondly, then dug a cell phone out of her pocket. "I'll call over there with my credit card info right now so all you have to do is pick me out a couple of shirts in some nice colors."

"Sure," Kate said. Out of the corner of her eye, she watched Jamie nod good-bye to the other trainer, then disappear in the direction of the rings. "What size do you need?"

Ten minutes later, Kate was stepping into the airy tent that housed the largest tack and apparel vendor at the show. Her shopping list was a little longer than it had started out. After giving Kate her size, Mrs. Walsh had decided she might as well get *three* new show shirts, just in case. And a package of hairnets. A crop to replace the one her horse had stepped on. Some boot socks and a spare set of laces.

It didn't take Kate long to pick up the smaller stuff. Then

she stepped over to the rack of show shirts. There were dozens of them in every color imaginable. Kate started checking tags, grabbing the first three shirts she found in the right size. Mrs. Walsh hadn't seemed to care much about colors, and Kate didn't have time to play fashion adviser.

She headed toward the register, squeezing past a rack of breeches. Then paused, running her hand over the tidy row of Tailored Sportsmans, admiring the luxurious feel of the fabric. Her fingers caught on the tag of one pair, and when Kate looked, she realized it was the size she needed, one size smaller than her old breeches.

She stared at the tag, particularly the price—more than she'd paid for any single item of clothing in her life. If only she were like Zara and Tommi and Fitz and Mrs. Walsh; if only she could afford to drop a couple hundred bucks without blinking an eye.

She glanced down at the pile of items in her arms, then back at the breeches. Before she quite knew what she was doing, she'd grabbed the hanger and slung the pants over her arm. A moment later she was dropping the whole lot on the counter.

"Will that be all?" the bored-looking twentysomething salesgirl asked.

"Yes," Kate said in a voice that sounded strange to her own ears. "Charge it to Mrs. Elaine Walsh's account, please."

Tommi had just put Legs in the cross-ties and stepped back to peel off her gloves when someone clapped his hands over her eyes.

"Hey!" she blurted out, startled. "Fitz, if that's you, I swear I'm going to kick you in the—"

"Surprise!" a voice interrupted. "It's not Fitz, it's me."

"Alex!" Tommi pushed his hands away, then spun around. "Oh my God, I can't believe it! What are you doing here?"

He grinned, looking pleased with himself. "I was bored, I missed you, so I decided to drive up and surprise you. And it was totally worth it. You look super sexy in your riding getup." His eyes slid appreciatively up and down her body before returning to her face. "Happy to see me?"

"Are you kidding? Of course!" Tommi wasn't quite sure what to think. She tilted her head back as he came in for a kiss. "I can't believe you came all the way up here, though."

He kissed her again, then grabbed both her hands in his. "I told you, I missed you. And I'd rather drive up to steal a few minutes with you than spend another boring weekend in the Hamptons playing tennis with Parker."

Tommi smiled. "Really?"

"Uh-huh." He grinned and squeezed her hands. "So now that I'm here, can I take you to lunch? I passed this cool-looking little burger joint on my way through town."

"Um . . ." Tommi glanced at Legs. She'd just finished lunge-ing him, and he was still sweaty and blowing a bit. Her plan had been to bring him into the barn just long enough to remove his boots, then hose him off and walk him out.

Alex dropped her hands, then reached into his shorts pocket and pulled out his car keys. "Come on, say yes," he wheedled. "I'll drive."

Just then Miguel came down the aisle. "Hey, are you busy

right now?" Tommi called to him. "I was just about to cool Legs out, but—"

"You need me to take him?" the groom finished for her with his usual good-natured smile. "Sure, I can do that."

Tommi smiled back. "Thanks, Miguel. You're the best."

"*Sí*, that's what they tell me." The groom winked at her, then turned to give Legs a pat. "Wanna go for a walk, big boy?"

Tommi felt a twinge of guilt, knowing that Miguel was busy enough without her suddenly adding an extra task to his workload. But Alex had driven all the way up here just to see her. How could she say no to that?

Soon she was in the tack stall, changing out of her boots. While she searched for a pair of sandals in her bag, Alex poked around the place, checking out the framed photos and the multicolored mass of ribbons hanging overhead. "Looks like you guys win a lot," he said. "So does everyone from the barn come to these shows?"

"Not everyone, but most." Tommi finally located the sandals under her spare breeches. "Jamie has an assistant trainer who stays home to take care of the horses and riders who aren't showing."

"Hmm." He stared up at a photo of Jamie. "So what about your friends? You know—the kids you ride with in your group lessons. Are they all here?"

"Yeah." Tommi shot him a quick look, pretty sure she knew why he'd asked. Was he hoping for a chance to schmooze Zara some more? Was that the real reason he'd driven all the way up here?

She banished the thought immediately. She so wasn't that

girl. If he said he'd come to see her, she was willing to take him at his word.

Besides, so what if he was hoping to take advantage of her friendship with Zara to finagle a meeting with Zac? It was called networking, and it was a big part of what made the world go round. Sort of like her father's standing tennis date with the mayor. Sure, her dad liked tennis. He probably even liked the mayor. That didn't change the fact that being on a first-name basis benefitted both of them.

Alex had liked Tommi before he ever found out she rode with Zara, so it wasn't as if he was using her. So he was ambitious, so what? So was she. Wasn't that the whole reason she was driving herself nuts over this Legs deal?

"I'm ready," she said, sliding her sandals on and standing up. "Let's go—I'm famished."

"Are you okay? I sort of feel like I'm talking to myself."

Tommi blinked, snapping out of her thoughts. Glancing across the table, she saw Alex staring at her. The two of them were in a greasy but picturesque little burger place in the equally picturesque upstate town near the showgrounds. Alex's bacon cheddar burger was half gone, but Tommi had barely taken three bites of her avocado and Swiss.

"Oh, man," she said, shaking her head. "I'm really sorry. Guess I just have a lot on my mind."

"Like what?" Alex shrugged. "I mean, I'm no Dr. Phil, but I'm a pretty good listener if you need to talk it out or whatever."

"It's not really that big a deal." Tommi picked up her burger and stared at it. "No, I'm lying. It kind of is a big deal. At least to me."

"Yeah?" he prompted.

She sighed. "It's Legs," she said, setting the burger down again. "This girl from a barn up in Boston saw me warming him up the other day, and . . ."

She went on to tell him the whole story. Vanessa. The test ride. The horse's reaction to her.

". . . so it's been a whole day, and I haven't heard a peep from her or her trainer," she finished. "I'm starting to wonder if she changed her mind." She bit her lip. "Actually, I'm sort of hoping she did. That way the decision's out of my hands."

Alex raised an eyebrow. "You never struck me as a girl who's afraid of making a decision."

"Usually I'm not." Tommi grimaced. "But this time I feel like either decision is going to be wrong, no matter what."

Alex grabbed his soda and took a sip, looking thoughtful. "Okay," he said, setting the glass down. "So if you sell him to her and it doesn't work out, is that going to ruin your rep? You know—screw up your good name for this whole horse-selling deal?"

"Maybe," Tommi said quickly, realizing he could be right. Was this what her instincts had been telling her all along? That this deal, no matter how convenient, wasn't worth the potential fallout?

But just as quickly, she realized she was grasping at straws. That wasn't why she was resisting the deal, and she knew it.

"Actually, I doubt it," she corrected herself. "I mean, sure, it would be great if the first horse I sell goes on to great things.

But like I said, Vanessa has quite the rep already. Nobody's going to blame me—or the horse—if she fails with him. It might even work out for the best if someone else in her barn ends up with the ride—maybe even her trainer."

Alex nodded. "That's good. So this really could be your chance to clean up on this deal, impress your father, and move on to bigger and better things."

"I guess." Tommi picked up her burger and took a bite, then chewed slowly as she thought about it. After she swallowed, she shook her head. "I don't know, though. I keep getting stuck on the idea that Vanessa so obviously isn't a good match for Legs, even though she doesn't seem to realize it. If she buys him, I just know they'll both end up frustrated."

"So what? It'll be her problem, not yours."

"Yeah." Tommi picked at a blob of cheese on her plate. "But Legs is such a cool horse—he deserves better."

"And you said he'll probably get it once she gets tired of him, right?" Alex leaned forward and gazed at her. "Look, you can't get caught up in all the what-ifs, okay? You need to do what's best for *you*. Because if you think about it, you really can't control anyone except yourself anyway. And once you sell a horse, it's out of your hands no matter what. Right?"

"Right."

"So why stress about it?" He sat back in his seat and smiled. "Just do what you need to do to make your own dreams happen, and let the rest take care of itself."

She thought about that for a second, then smiled back. "Maybe you're right," she said. "You're not so bad at this Dr. Phil stuff after all. Thanks."

Alex reached across the table and took her hand in his. "You're welcome."

She squeezed his hand, grateful that he'd talked her into coming out to lunch, and even more grateful that he cared enough to talk this out with her. Okay, so maybe she still wasn't sure what she was going to do. But he'd made her feel a little better about even considering sending Legs off with Vanessa. *If* she even still wanted to buy him, that is.

It wasn't easy to eat the rest of her lunch with one hand tucked into Alex's. But Tommi managed.

"Watch out for the rollback, it rides trickier than it walks," Tommi said to Kate as she rode past.

Kate nodded her thanks, too anxious to speak. Tommi had just finished the course on her eq horse. Now it was Kate's turn.

"Ready?" Jamie asked, giving Fable a pat on her neck.

Again, Kate just nodded. Gathering up her reins, she glanced around. Tommi had dismounted and was running up her stirrups; Elliot was standing by, waiting to take the horse from her. Marissa was mounted on her own horse nearby, her face a mask of sheer panic as it always was before an eq class. Zara, Dani, and a few of the other people from the barn were standing at the rail. Tommi's new boyfriend was there, too, standing by Zara, though for some reason Kate couldn't come up with his name just then. And of course Fitz had just ridden over from the warm-up ring on his eq horse. He wasn't going until after Kate and Marissa finished, but Kate knew he didn't want to miss her ride.

"Ready," she finally managed to croak out at Jamie, even though she was feeling anything but.

She nudged Fable with her calves to send him in through the open gate. As it swung shut behind them, she heard someone—Dani, she guessed—yell "Go, Kate!"

Fable was alert and jigging right away, his ears pricked toward the fences. Kate sent him into a trot, and just like that, the ring came into focus.

That was good. She'd been in kind of a daze since leaving the tack tent a couple of hours earlier. That was the only explanation for everything that had happened since. She'd ducked into an empty stall to change into the new breeches, which fit pretty well. There hadn't been much time to think about it, since it was time to get ready for that schooling hunter division. Kate had asked Max to take Mrs. Walsh her new stuff, then dashed off to tack up.

She barely remembered the trips that had followed— outside line, diagonal, outside, diagonal, what was to remember, really? Luckily Jamie had already decided to skip the hack with both greenies, as there hadn't been time to do more than toss the reins at Javier before rushing off again to get Fable ready.

But now she was finally snapping out of it, and the more she forced herself to think about what she'd done, the more horrified she felt. How could she have done it? Just put the breeches on Mrs. Walsh's tab like that? It was stealing, and she knew it. What would her father say if he knew?

Still, this wasn't the moment to worry about it. Not with Fable feeling like a lit firecracker under her and the first fence of a tough eq course coming up fast. The best she could do was promise herself that she'd return the breeches right after she finished the eq. Somehow she'd avoided getting them dirty during the earlier rides despite her reputation for attracting manure stains and horse slobber. The tags and receipt were still in the front pocket. All she had to do was convince the clerk to take them back, and she could forget this had ever happened. She'd worry about tomorrow's classes later.

They were at the first fence. Fable leaped over it and surged forward on the landing. When Kate half-halted, he responded with a playful little buck.

"Easy," Kate murmured. She could already tell that she couldn't go on autopilot as she had with those greenies. Fable was feeling extra strong today. Time to pay attention and ride.

Halfway through the course, she was already exhausted from holding him together. As he cantered around a corner, pulling to the inside, she tried to ignore that her arms were shaking and her legs felt like jelly. Just a few more jumps, and they'd be done.

Fable pricked his ears toward a big oxer, but maintained a steady pace and cleared it handily. He shook his head on the sharp turn to the in-and-out, but listened to Kate's aids and got through that just fine, too. Two more to go.

The second-to-last fence was a narrow gate. Kate saw that they were coming in a little strong and half-halted, reeling him in a bit. The horse shook his head again, swishing his tail in annoyance. He slowed as she asked, but she could feel his muscles coiling like a spring. Uh-oh.

Sure enough, the horse put in an extra-big effort as he left the ground. Kate tried to hold her position, but the back-cracking jump sent her lurching forward onto Fable's neck. She grabbed for his mane as he started the downward arc, but her fingers couldn't seem to grasp the tiny, slippery braids. She fought for balance and managed to stay aboard as Fable's front hooves hit the ground. But when she tried to push herself back, get her butt in the saddle where it belonged, she saw spots dancing in front of her eyes, bright and sparkly like silver fire-flies. The whole world started to tilt sideways, and then every-thing went black.

NINETEEN

— — — — —

"Oh my God!" someone yelled. Zara wasn't sure, but she thought it might have been her.

But they were all staring at the same thing. Kate hitting the ground hard and just lying there.

Fitz was already off his horse and running for the gate. Tommi was right behind him. Zara followed them, pushing past Tommi's annoying friend Alex.

"Move," she ordered him, in no mood to be polite.

"Wait," Marissa said, grabbing Zara by the arm before she could follow the others. She'd slid down from her horse, too, tossing the reins to Max. "We can't all run in there."

Zara glanced into the ring, realizing she was right. Tommi and Fitz were already at Kate's side, along with Jamie. What more could Zara do? It wasn't as if she knew first aid or any crap like that. It wasn't even as if she and Kate were such good friends. Come to think of it, she was supposed to be pissed at the girl right now for that glove thing.

But she couldn't muster up much anger as she stared at Kate lying there in the sand like some limp old rag doll. What was going on with her, anyway? That whole glove incident had been totally weird. Especially the way Kate had looked when Zara had busted her, sort of wild-eyed and gaunt and desperate. And now this.

The crowd was murmuring with concern, while the announcer called for the paramedics to please come to the equitation ring.

Marissa herded Zara back to the others, making soothing noises at all of them. Playing mother hen. That seemed to be her thing.

Summer chose that moment to ride over from the direction of the warm-up ring. She was supposed to ride after Fitz.

"What's going on?" she asked, pulling her horse to a halt.

"Kate came off," Marissa said. "I guess Fable jumped her loose, and she couldn't hold on."

Dani shook her head. "I think there was more to it than that," she declared. "I mean, since when can't Kate ride a big jump? It looked like she, like, passed out or something!"

Zara glanced at the ring again. Miguel had appeared out of nowhere and caught Fable. Meanwhile Kate had actually managed to sit up, with Fitz and Jamie supporting her on either side.

The others were still chattering excitedly, but Zara stayed silent as she watched Tommi take Kate by the hand, helping her to her feet. The ring's reddish-brown footing was ground into Kate's clothes from head to foot.

As she stared at the other girl's lean frame, her bony wrists sticking out from the sleeves of her jacket, Zara started to wonder if Dani was right, if something was seriously wrong here. Was it possible that Kate could be anorexic or something, and none of them had even noticed?

"Knock, knock," Tommi called out as she pushed open the door to the hotel room Kate was sharing with Dani. "Can I come in?"

Kate looked up. She was sitting cross-legged on her bed, dressed in baggy sweatpants and a T-shirt.

"Sure," she said. "But don't come too close. I might be contagious."

Tommi studied her face. Jamie and most of the others seemed perfectly willing to believe Kate's story about having a virus or something. And in a way, it did make sense. It certainly explained Kate's scary fall in the eq ring yesterday, along with her paleness and generally unhealthy look the past week or so.

But Tommi wasn't so sure. Call it a hunch.

"So when did you feel yourself getting sick?" she asked, perching on the edge of the bed.

"Oh, I don't know," Kate said vaguely, waving a hand. "You know how it is at shows. I was so busy I probably didn't pay attention soon enough."

"So do you think it's, like, a stomach bug or something? Could it be food poisoning?" Tommi asked. "What did you eat yesterday?"

"I don't really remember, but yeah, maybe. Anyway, I'm already feeling better," Kate said. "Jamie's making me stay here and rest, though. I just hope things aren't too crazy today being one person short. At least it's the last day."

"I'm sure we'll manage." Tommi felt troubled as she stared at her friend. She could tell that Kate wasn't telling her the truth. At least not the whole truth. What was really going on here?

Kate was picking at her fingernails, not looking at Tommi. Her blue eyes were anxious and distant.

"Look, Kate," Tommi blurted out, unable to hold it in any longer. "You'd tell me if something was really wrong, right? I mean, you know you can trust me."

Kate's head shot up; the startled look in her eyes reminded Tommi of the time she'd almost hit a dog with her car. It had looked at her the exact same way before darting to the curb just in time.

"I—I . . . ," Kate began, then gulped. "Look, you can't tell anyone, okay?"

"Swear." Tommi held her breath, not wanting to push too hard.

Kate bit her lip so hard it left a dent. "I really screwed up," she said, her voice barely above a whisper. "I—I stole something. A brand-new pair of Tailored Sportsmans."

Whatever Tommi had been expecting to hear, that definitely wasn't it. "Huh?" she said. "What do you mean, you stole them?"

"My show breeches got ruined, and then Mrs. Walsh sent me to pick up some stuff for her at the vendor's tent, and I saw the breeches there and just sort of added them to the pile without thinking." Kate took a long, shuddering breath, clutching the bedspread in both hands so tightly that her knuckles were white. "And now they're ruined, too, so I can't take them back, and there's no way I can ever pay for them before Mrs. Walsh finds out, and—"

"Wait." Tommi was having trouble following this. "So you charged a pair of breeches to Mrs. Walsh's account—the ones you were wearing when you fell yesterday?"

"Uh-huh." Kate looked sick. "I know it was wrong. I have no idea what got into me, I guess I was so desperate I wasn't thinking."

"But what happened to your other breeches?" Tommi asked.

Kate shrugged, her gaze skittering away and focusing on the hotel room wall. "I, um, spilled Thrush Buster all down the front of them when I was treating that new import horse with the bad feet," she said. "You know how that stuff stains. It's not like I could go into the ring with big purple blotches all over my pants."

That part wasn't so hard to believe. Kate was famous for focusing more on keeping the horses' turnout spotless than her own.

"Okay," Tommi said. "So why didn't you just tell someone? Me, for instance? You know I would've helped you out."

She had to admit it, she was a little hurt. They were supposed to be friends. Tommi wouldn't hesitate to go to Kate for help, advice, whatever. Didn't Kate feel the same way?

"I don't know," Kate whispered.

"It's not like I couldn't have spotted you the cash for a new pair," Tommi went on. "Or just got them for you as an early birthday present or something. And actually, I bet Mrs. Walsh would've bought them for you if you'd just asked her. You've done her enough favors over the years, helping out with her horses and stuff."

Kate just shrugged. "Too late now. I've got to tell her the truth and figure out a way to pay her back." Her eyes filled with tears. "I hope she isn't too mad; I never meant to hurt her."

"You didn't hurt her," Tommi said. "If you didn't tell her, she'd probably never even notice the extra charge. An extra pair of breeches to her is like, I don't know, the cost of a DVD or something would be to most people."

That didn't seem to make Kate feel any better. She just sniffled, then hid her head in her hands.

Tommi slid onto the bed and put an arm around her. "Look, I'm sorry," she said. "I've got to go. But I'll help you fix this, okay? I'll tell Mrs. Walsh, um, that I asked you to pick up those breeches for me, and things got confused. I pay her back, and it's all good. How's that sound?"

Kate sniffled again and looked up. "Really?" she said. "You'd do that, even after I screwed up so badly?"

"Of course." Tommi hugged her. "Just stop beating yourself up, okay? Everyone makes mistakes. I'll take care of it."

Tommi was still distracted as she hurried into the hotel restaurant. Even if it made her a little late, she figured she'd better grab something to eat before she headed over to the show. It would be a long day, and she definitely didn't want to face it on an empty stomach.

She grabbed a tray and headed for the breakfast buffet. When she got there, she found Zara poring over the selection of pastries. "Oh, good," Zara said when she saw her. "At least if I'm late, I won't be the only one."

— 223 —

"Exactly what I was thinking." Tommi forced a wan smile.

Zara glanced past Tommi. "That dork boyfriend of yours still around?"

"No," Tommi said. "He drove home last night."

"Good." Zara looked relieved. "I was really hoping he wasn't going to be riding back down to the city with us. The boy's cute and all, but man, was he bugging the shit out of me yesterday. Practically invited himself to move in with me once Zac gets back from Europe."

Tommi shrugged, too distracted to worry about it. Okay, so maybe Alex was taking this whole networking thing a little too far. She was sure Zara had dealt with worse.

"Sorry," she said, stepping past Zara so she could reach the toast. "He's really into music. Wants to get into producing or something when he's older."

"Whatever." Zara didn't sound too interested as she grabbed a cherry Danish. "You check in on Kate this morning?"

Tommi shot her a wary look. "Yeah," she said. "Why?"

"Just wondering. She looked pretty wiped out yesterday." Zara picked up her tray. "Way more than I'd expect after a pretty ordinary slide-and-flop fall. I just wondered if, you know, there was something else going on with her. And I'm not talking about having the sniffles or whatever she's claiming."

"Something else?" Tommi's voice came out sharper than she'd intended. "What do you mean?"

Zara frowned. "Don't bite my head off, okay? If you don't want to talk about it, we won't talk about it."

"Talk about what?" Tommi grabbed a bowl of fruit salad, then followed the other girl toward an out-of-the-way table.

Zara set down her tray, then flopped into a chair. "Look, I haven't said anything to anyone else," she said. "I didn't want to be, you know, a gossip or something. But come on—you must've noticed Kate's looking paler and skinnier than ever lately. Then there's that fall. Don't tell me you'd expect her to come off just because her horse overjumped a little."

"She was probably just nervous." Tommi sat down across from the other girl. "She hasn't been doing the Big Eq for long. Maybe she tensed up too much trying to hold her position."

"Maybe." Zara sounded skeptical. "Or maybe she's got something else going on that's making her too weak to hold on."

"Like the flu?" Tommi said, not really wanting to know what Zara was thinking. Even though she sort of already did.

"Like an eating disorder," Zara said bluntly. "Don't tell me it hasn't occurred to you, too. I know you're not that stupid."

Tommi wanted to leap to Kate's defense, to deny it. But when she got right down to it, she had to admit Zara wasn't wrong.

"I don't know," she said slowly. "I mean, we shouldn't jump to any conclusions. It might just be a stomach bug or something after all, right? But—" Just then her phone went off in her pocket. "Excuse me," she muttered, digging it out. The return number was one she didn't recognize. "Hello?" she said.

"Tommi? This is Abby Durand-Evans."

Tommi's heart skipped a beat. In all the drama over Kate's fall, she'd almost forgotten that she still hadn't heard back from Vanessa. "Oh—hello," she said. "I mean yes, this is Tommi. How are you?"

"Fine, fine." The trainer sounded rushed. "Listen, sorry

we didn't get back to you sooner. Had some trouble reaching Vanessa's folks—they're traveling in Nepal or somewhere crazy like that."

"Oh," Tommi said. She clutched the phone more tightly to her ear, ignoring Zara's curious stare. "That's okay, no problem."

"The wait was worth it, though," the trainer went on. "Vanessa loved the horse, and is willing to pay your full asking price as long as he vets. Actually we were hoping to close the deal today so we can take him home with us from the show."

"Oh! Wow." Tommi swallowed hard, her mind racing.

Vanessa wanted Legs. Right now. No haggling. It was like her father's dream come true. He'd probably be so thrilled he'd be willing to help Tommi buy another prospect right away. By the end of the summer she could have two or three sales under her belt, maybe, and then there'd be no way he wouldn't let her keep at it over her senior year. And after that? Well, she would have to see. But at least she'd be off to a good start.

Then her mind flashed to the image of Vanessa riding Legs. Hauling on his mouth. The confused, unhappy look in the horse's eyes. How long could he put up with that? Was it fair to make him try?

Tommi closed her eyes for a second, knowing the trainer was waiting for her response. She knew what her father would tell her to say. Probably Alex, too. Maybe even Jamie.

But she found herself wondering—WWKD? What would Kate do? For all her current issues, whatever they might be, Kate was one of the truest horsemen Tommi knew. She sort of wished she could put Vanessa's trainer on hold for a few minutes, then run back to Kate's room and discuss it with her.

Was that even necessary, though? Even though Kate might have been struggling with some serious problems right under her nose, giving Tommi the uneasy feeling that she didn't know her anywhere near as well as she'd thought, Tommi *did* know what her friend would say about this. Some things weren't about the money.

"Sorry," she said into the phone. "I, uh, was just about to call you to let you know. I've decided to keep Legs in training a little longer before I sell him. I just don't feel comfortable with where he is yet, and I'd like to get him going a little more solidly before I let him go."

"What?" The trainer sounded surprised and a little put out. "Are you saying you don't want to sell the horse?"

"Yeah," Tommi said. "Sorry to have wasted your time."

"I'm sorry, too." The trainer's voice was clipped and tight. "Good-bye."

Tommi didn't have a chance to say anything else before the line cut off. She couldn't really blame the trainer for being annoyed. And she didn't even want to think about how Vanessa would react when she found out.

But she couldn't quite find it in her to care. She was the only one who needed to face herself in the mirror every day, and she just couldn't do that if she sold a horse like Legs into a situation where he was set up for failure from the start. Even if nobody else blamed her when things went south, she'd blame herself.

"What was all that about?" Zara asked through a mouthful of gooey pastry.

Tommi had almost forgotten she was there. She told her the gist of what had just happened. "Sorry, guess that means you won't be getting your commission," she joked weakly.

"Bummer," Zara said. "But don't sweat it. That girl seemed like a royal beyotch. Legs is too good for someone like her."

"Definitely." Tommi smiled. "And it's not like I don't still have plenty of time to find a better match for him. In the meantime, what my dad doesn't know won't hurt me, right?"

TWENTY

Tommi slammed on the brakes as a taxi cut her off right outside the Holland Tunnel. "Asshole," she muttered. Then she glanced at Zara, who was slumped in the passenger seat, staring out at the multicolored lights of lower Manhattan. "Sorry about that."

"Whatever." Zara yawned. "Just try not to crash before you drop me off, okay?"

Tommi rolled her eyes. "I'll do my best." She spun the wheel, taking the turn onto Sixth Avenue. "So what are we going to do about Kate?"

Zara just shrugged. When Tommi looked over again, the other girl looked bored. No wonder. The two of them had spent the better part of the long Sunday-evening drive back from the show discussing Kate, but hadn't come close to any solutions. All Tommi knew was that she was worried about her friend. Really worried. What if she *was* spiraling into anorexia or something?

It seemed crazy. But it also kind of didn't. Kate had always been majorly intense, all about staying in control, always being perfect. Wasn't that pretty much a recipe for those kinds of problems?

"Maybe we need to talk to her," she said. "Get her to admit what's going on, if anything is."

"You mean like an intervention or something?" Zara shot her a look. "Not sure I'm up for that much drama."

"Fine, if you don't want to help, then don't," Tommi snapped. "*I'm* not planning to abandon my friend when she's in trouble. So sue me."

"Big talk for someone who didn't even admit her *friend* had a problem until I brought it up," Zara shot back. "Anyway, since when are Kate and I BFFs? She sure didn't act like it when she tried to sneak around behind my back and pawn those gloves I bought her."

"Cut her a break," Tommi said, wanting to defend Kate but definitely not about to spill all her secrets to Zara. "You don't know why she did that. Maybe she had a good reason."

"Yeah. Like turning me into her personal cash machine. Cha-ching!"

"Whatever," Tommi muttered. "Let's not talk about it anymore. I need to pay attention to the traffic anyhow."

Zara was glad to see her building appear on the next block. It had been a long drive back from the show. *Really* long. Tommi had spent the entire time chewing over Kate's possible problems as obsessively as Chaucer gnawed on his rawhide bone.

Not that Zara didn't get where she was coming from. If their suspicions were right, this was a big freaking deal. But Zara wasn't really used to worrying that much about someone else's life, and she was tired from the long weekend of showing and not in the mood right now.

"Here we are," Tommi said, pulling to the curb behind a parked van. "And listen, sorry if I was a little cranky before. I'm just worried about Kate, and it's stressing me out, you know?"

"Yeah. Me too." Zara shot her a small, cautious smile. "Thanks for the ride. I'll see you Tuesday."

Tommi nodded. "Maybe we can figure something out by then. I'll text you if I come up with anything, okay?"

"Okay, cool." Zara climbed out of the car, grabbed her bag out of the backseat, and headed inside.

As she rode up in the elevator, she braced herself for party central. After leaving Stacie alone for the entire long weekend, she figured it was lucky the building was still intact. She wasn't even going to try to guess what the inside of the loft looked like by now. Or how many of Stacie's new "friends" were in there right this second, trashing the place even further.

The elevator doors slid open, and Zara stepped out onto the landing. To her surprise, it was quiet—no pounding music, no muffled voices or screams of laughter coming from behind the door.

"Weird," she muttered, fishing for her key.

She pushed the door open and stepped inside the silent apartment. All the lights were on, and the place was an even bigger mess than usual. Zara stepped over a crumpled beer can, wrinkling her nose. No way was she cleaning up this shit.

"Stacie?" she called. "You home?"

There was no answer. Zara picked her way through the discarded cans, bottles, cigarette butts, and other debris into the main area. She had a pretty strong stomach, but the stink was already getting to her—a rank combination of stale smoke, stale beer, bad cologne, and old puke.

"Hope she's out buying cleaning stuff," Zara muttered as she noticed the source of the puke smell, a half-dried splat on the floor near the TV. Gross. Wherever Stacie was, she'd better get back soon and deal with the mess she'd created.

Zara stepped back to the foyer to deposit her boots under the ledge in the message center. As she did, she noticed a note stuck to the schedule board. When she grabbed it, she saw that it was from her cousin.

Hope you had a fun show, Z! it read in Stacie's big, loopy handwriting. *I'm going away for a week or so—Steve wants to take me to his family's place in the mountains. Isn't that romantic? See u when I get back, prolly end of next w/e or so. Ciao! XXXOOO*

Zara gritted her teeth, then crumpled the note in her hand. Great. Just great. So Cousin Stacie trashes the place, then skips town with some random guy Zara never even heard of? Fabulous.

"Whatever," Zara muttered. Noticing that the message light on the phone was blinking, she punched the button with a little more force than necessary. There were more than a dozen messages. Most were skippable—boring stuff from Zac's lawyers or moronic interviewers who hadn't yet figured out he was touring or whatever. She fast-forwarded through those quickly, then stopped on the second-to-last message when she heard her father's familiar voice.

"*How's it going, Little Z?*" Zac sounded cheerful. And maybe a little drunk. "*Things are cool over here—European fans are awesome. Anyway, hope you and Stacie are good. Give me a call back whenever if you want.*"

That was it. Zara hit delete, then kept her finger hovering over the button, waiting for the last message. It was another familiar voice.

"*Zara, love, it's Mom!*" Gina sang out. "*It's Sunday morning early, and I'm sure you're still at your show—that was this weekend, wasn't it? In any case, I have some fabulous news. Well, more of a silver lining, really.*" Her musical laugh tinkled out of the tiny speaker. "*Remember how I told you we were having permit problems here? Well, it looks like there's going to be a longer delay than they thought, so we've got some unexpected time off. And what better way for me to fill it than by popping home to New York to visit with my darling baby girl? I just booked the flight—I'll be there in time for lunch on Tuesday. Can't wait to see you, my love!*"

Zara froze, trying to process what her mother had said. Tuesday. Here. Gina was coming here. In less than two days.

She turned and stared out at the disaster that was the loft. Great. Just freaking great.

Kate still felt kind of shaky when she arrived at the barn on Monday morning. It had been a rough weekend, but she just wanted to put it behind her and move on. As much as possible, anyway. Tommi had covered for her with Mrs. Walsh as promised, though Kate couldn't help wondering exactly how long it would take her to pay her friend back for those expensive breeches. She knew Tommi wouldn't care if it took a year—or if she ever paid her back at all, for that matter—but somehow that made it even worse.

She was surprised to see a couple of familiar cars in the parking lot. Most of the other juniors stayed away on Mondays, since the barn was supposed to be closed to clients. Especially the Monday after a show, when Jamie preferred to give most of the horses a well-deserved day off. But there was Tommi's car, and Fitz's right next to it.

Anxiety fluttered in the pit of Kate's stomach as she cut her engine. She'd managed to convince Jamie that she'd just had a mild flu or something. But she wasn't sure her friends believed her—she'd noticed Tommi and Zara giving her weird looks when she'd dragged herself over to the showgrounds on Sunday afternoon to watch Jamie ride in the Grand Prix, where he'd come in fourth on a client's new horse. At the time she hadn't worried too much about what they might be thinking. All she'd had on her mind was surviving the rest of the weekend, then going home and sleeping for about twenty-four hours straight.

But now here she was, and it looked as if she might have to face them sooner than she'd planned. She just hoped they didn't overreact to what had happened. Anyone could get overtired and run down, right?

As soon as she stepped into the barn, she saw Tommi and Zara sitting on one of the benches. They were obviously waiting for her, judging by the way they leaped to their feet and hurried over.

"Kate!" Tommi said. "How are you?"

"Fine!" Kate made her voice as cheery as she could manage. "What are you guys doing here? Never mind, don't tell me—too much to do."

"Not so fast." Tommi grabbed her by the arm as she tried to hurry past. "We need to talk to you."

Kate pulled back, but her friend's grip was strong. "Can it wait?" she asked. "I should really go see if the guys need my help cleaning out the trailers."

"No, this definitely can't wait," Tommi said.

"Yeah. Besides, I can't stay long," Zara added, checking her watch. "Actually, I can't believe I got up this early. I need to get back to the city soon to meet the cleaning service—God, I hope they weren't lying when they claimed they work fast! And while I'm at it, maybe I should start working on finding a detective who specializes in missing persons of the idiotic variety."

Kate had no idea what she was talking about, but didn't have the mental energy to worry about it. "Listen," she told Zara, "if this is about the glove thing, I'm really sorry. It's just that Summer really wanted them, and I just thought—"

"Forget it," Zara interrupted, waving a hand. "Not a big deal. Anyway, I should've guessed it was all Summer's fault somehow. The girl's a major pain in the ass."

Kate was relieved that she didn't seem mad anymore. Meanwhile Tommi was still dragging her down the aisle toward a deserted storage room.

Once inside, Kate turned to face the other two. "Well?" she said.

There was a moment of silence. Tommi and Zara traded a glance, both of them looking uncomfortable. "Well . . . ," Tommi began, then stopped.

"Um, yeah," Zara said. "Listen, we . . ."

Her voice trailed off, too. Despite her own anxiety, Kate couldn't help a flicker of amusement as she glanced at the two of them. Tommi was always so confident, so on top of things, Zara so carelessly cool and mouthy. It wasn't every day anyone got to see that particular pair struck speechless.

"Okay, here's the thing," Tommi blurted out at last, sounding almost angry. "We're really worried about you, Kate. We know you always work really hard and all, but lately you've been pushing yourself way too hard. Like, beyond the breaking point."

Zara nodded. "Exhibit A? That crazy fall on Saturday. Jamie might believe it was the flu taking you out, but we know better."

"What are you talking about?" Kate shrugged, inching toward the door. "It's not like I usually go around passing out for no reason. It had to be the flu. No biggie—I took a bunch of vitamin C when I got home, and I feel fine now."

"Vitamin C, huh?" Zara's green eyes slid from Kate's face to her body. "Eat anything else lately? I'm thinking no."

"Zara!" Tommi frowned at her, then turned to Kate. "Look, Kate. If you're so busy you forget to eat, that's one thing, but if there's something else going on, you need to, like, get some help before it goes any further."

"What?" Kate's eyes widened as she caught on to what they were saying. "Are you guys insane? How could you even think something like that?" She glared at Tommi. "Especially you! I thought you knew me better than that."

She spun around and rushed toward the door. Tommi took two quick steps and caught her by the wrist again.

"Wait," she said. "I'm sorry, Kate. But we had to ask. We care about you, okay?"

"Yeah. I knew some girls in LA with eating disorders," Zara put in. "It wasn't pretty."

"Whatever. I don't have time to stand around listening to your stupid conspiracy theories." Kate yanked her arm loose from Tommi's grip. "And I'm not about to start blaming my own mistakes on some stupid made-up eating disorder or whatever. Maybe that's how things work in your celebrity-rehab rich people's world. But I'm not like that. I'm handling it, okay? It's all under control."

She stormed out of the storage room before Tommi and Zara could decide to diagnose her with some other horrible thing. Her mind was churning so much that she didn't notice Fitz coming toward her until he called her name.

"I was hoping I'd run into you," he said cheerfully, his words coming out a little too loud and fast, like they always did when he was overly distracted or keyed up about something. "Didn't want to text you in case you were home, still sleeping it off or whatever. How're you doing? Feeling better?"

"Um, yeah," Kate said cautiously. Was Fitz about to get on her case now, too? If so, he seemed weirdly happy about it.

"Good. You scared me when you came tumbling off that

horse." He reached out and squeezed her arm. "So what do you think? Is it safe to kiss you, or are you still contagious?"

"I don't think I'm contagious." Kate was relieved. So he bought the flu story. Good. Yeah, she was really trying to be honest with him and all, but it was easier just to go with that than try to make him understand that the stress and lack of sleep had just caught up with her. Especially since even Tommi obviously couldn't comprehend it.

Fitz gave her a quick peck on the lips. "Excellent, because not being able to kiss you all day yesterday was torture," he said with a grin. "But listen, before I get, like, lost in your lips and forget everything else, I have some big news I've been dying to share with you. I got a new horse!"

"What?" Kate was distracted, her mind already wandering back to the confrontation with Tommi and Zara. "You mean Ford?"

"No, not him. A totally new one, for real. He was delivered over the weekend while we were all away at the show." Fitz grabbed her hand. "Want to come meet him?"

If this was a joke, Kate didn't get it. Had he really bought a new horse? She hadn't heard anything about it.

He pulled her along the aisle. "He's going to be kind of a project," he said. "I'm hoping you'll help me out with him."

They stopped in front of a stall. Kate gasped as she recognized the rather scrawny head and neck hanging out over the stall guard. The horse's dull chestnut coat and ribby barrel stood out among the gleaming, fit show horses.

"Oh my God!" she exclaimed. "Is that Nat's horse?"

"Not anymore." Fitz grinned. "Flame's all mine now. When I saw how impressed you were with him, I figured you'd have a blast helping bring him along, polish up that diamond in the rough." He shrugged. "Best part is, he was so cheap I didn't even have to ask my folks for the money to buy him. I figure I'll just deal with the surprise extra boarding fees later."

"Oh my God," Kate said again. Her mind seemed to be stuck in neutral, and she couldn't quite take in what this meant.

Fitz seemed pleased by her stunned expression. "Anyway, I have plenty of horses to ride already, so I'm hoping you'll do most of the training and riding for me on this one," he said. "Once I clue my parents in, I'll make sure they work things out with Jamie so you even get a little cash out of the deal." He spun her to face him and wrapped his arms around her. "Surprised?" he asked.

"Yeah, that's an understatement." Kate forced a smile. It didn't take a genius to figure out that he'd done this all for her, risking still more parental wrath to make it happen. Another big, dramatic way to show he cared.

It was hard not to be flattered by that, especially after such a rotten weekend. But as Kate glanced at the tall chestnut gelding staring out of the stall at her, her stomach started doing nervous flips. Because she couldn't even begin to imagine what Nat was going to say about this.

Tommi wasn't sorry to see Zara leave a few minutes later. After overhearing Joy mention that she needed to drive over to the feed store, Zara had talked the assistant trainer into dropping her off at the nearest Metro North station on the way. Something about her cousin messing up the apartment; she'd spent most of the ride out to the barn blabbing about it, actually, though Tommi had been too worried about Kate to pay much attention.

And she was *still* worried about her. As soon as Zara was gone, Tommi went in search of Kate, hoping she'd cooled off by now. Their little intervention definitely hadn't gone as well as Tommi might have hoped. Had it been a huge mistake to ambush her like that? Kate might come across as meek and mild most of the time, but she'd just proved that it was possible to push her too far. Tommi needed to find her, make her understand that they were just trying to help. That they were worried about her—*really* worried.

She rounded the corner and spotted Kate halfway down the aisle with Fitz. The two of them were standing arm in arm in front of a stall, looking at a tall, lean chestnut Tommi didn't recognize. But she barely spared the horse a glance.

"Kate," she called out, hurrying toward them. "Can I talk to you a sec?"

She held her breath as Kate turned to face her. Her expression was guarded and anxious, but less angry than it had been earlier. Or was that wishful thinking?

"Yo, Tommi," Fitz said, gesturing toward the horse. "Check out my new ride."

"Later, okay?" Tommi didn't take her eyes off Kate. "I, um, really need Kate's advice about something."

"Uh-oh, sounds like girl stuff." Fitz laughed, clearly in one of his goofy, extra-happy moods and completely unaware of the tension. "Message received." He leaned down and planted a kiss atop Kate's blond head. "I'll wait for you out by the car, okay?"

"I'll be right there," Kate replied. "I'm sure this won't take long."

Fitz gave the chestnut a quick pat, then loped off down the aisle. As soon as he was out of sight, Tommi took a step forward.

"Listen, Kate," she said. "I'm really sorry Zara and I upset you."

"How could you do it, Tommi?" Kate said softly, her voice cracking a little. "It's bad enough you'd think something like that about me, without telling some girl I barely know all about it."

"Actually, Zara was the one who mentioned it to me first." Tommi shrugged. "But that doesn't really matter. Look, I know you're a superstrong person, Kate, and maybe I'm way out of line here. But it kind of freaked me out that you didn't come to me about the breeches thing, so I just want to say it now. If you're ever in trouble and need help, I've always got your back. Seriously. No limits."

Kate bit her lip, not quite meeting her eye. "I know you do," she whispered. "Thanks."

Tommi waited, hoping for more. But Kate was looking at her watch, maybe already thinking about taking off to meet Fitz.

"So," Tommi said quickly, not wanting her to go just yet. Things still felt way too unresolved, too uncertain. Definitely not Tommi's favorite feeling. "Who's this guy?" She stepped over to the chestnut, giving him a scratch on the neck as he nosed at her curiously.

"Fitz's new horse." Kate shot the gelding a look that Tommi couldn't quite figure out. "We saw him at the Happy Acres show last weekend, and, um, I mentioned that he looked pretty nice. So Fitz decided to buy him, and he wants me to help train him up into a show hunter."

"If Fitz was looking for a new horse, I wish he'd have told me. I have one I could've sold him." Tommi forced a grin, though she wasn't really in a joking mood. "But seriously, sounds like a cool project, I'm sure you'll have fun with him."

"Yeah." Kate didn't crack a smile. "Anyway, I should probably go—Fitz is taking me to the diner. You know, to celebrate."

"Oh." Tommi felt helpless, as if her friend was slipping away from her right in front of her eyes. How could she help if Kate wouldn't even talk to her? "Okay. Um, but maybe we could get together later? You know, just hang out—like old times. If you're up for it."

Kate had already started to turn away. But she paused, looking back at Tommi. "Sure," she said softly. "Maybe. That sounds nice, actually."

"Cool. I'll text you later." Tommi watched her hurry off down the aisle, still feeling worried—but also oddly relieved.

Okay, maybe the intervention had been a mistake. Maybe not. Either way, Tommi wasn't about to give up on her friend. Not now, not ever.

No limits.

The drama is far from over.

Read on for a sneak peek of the next

A CIRCUIT *novel*

ZARA

"So do you really think you can pull it off? Hide the whole Stacie thing from your mom?" Tommi asked.

"We'll find out, I guess." Zara was tired of talking about it. It was bad enough she had to live it. "Anyway, I figured I'd better come see my horses just in case I end up grounded for life or something."

Fitz grinned. "Whatever." He gave a light tug on the lead line as the tall, skinny chestnut gelding stretched his long neck toward the grass growing beside the path. "Come on, Kate, let's get our big boy inside and cleaned up."

"Yeah." Kate smiled and rubbed the horse's face as it turned and nuzzled at her. She looked even spacier than usual, and Zara wondered if she'd heard anything the rest of them had said in the past five minutes.

The barn's big double doors were standing open to catch whatever stray breeze might wander through to help the fans beat back the stifling August heat. Zara hung back to let the horse and his little band of groupies enter the barn first, then peeled off in the direction of Keeper's stall.

"Later," she called to the others, not bothering to wait for a response. Even though she was starting to think of them as friends, at least sort of, she didn't like to count on them feeling the same. Too easy to get knocked on your ass that way, and she had enough problems right now as it was.

As she rounded the corner, Zara checked her watch. Two thirty already. She'd have to hurry if she wanted to squeeze in a ride today. Or maybe she should just feed Keeper a few carrots and call it a day. She definitely wanted to be there when her mother got home that evening. Not that she had any clue what she was going to tell her this time . . .

"Zara! Oh good, you're here!"

Zara winced. Glancing over her shoulder, she saw Summer rushing toward her with a big, goofy grin on her face.

Summer skidded to a stop beside her. "Where were you yesterday?" she exclaimed. "You totally missed my big news! I'm having a Sweet Sixteen party at the Washington Crossing show! We're renting out, like, half the old mansion, and there's going to be a band and, like, a million guests and really awesome food and—"

"Yeah, I heard," Zara cut her off, putting as much excitement as she felt into her voice. Exactly none.

As usual, Summer didn't seem to notice. "Oh, you heard about it already? That's cool." She beamed. "I guess word spreads fast around here. Especially huge news like this, right? Anyway, you probably heard that, like, the whole barn is invited. But I wanted to make sure to invite you personally, you know? Oh! And there are going to be lots of adults there and stuff, so, like, if your parents wanted to come they're totally welcome, too."

Yeah. Of course they were. Zara could only imagine how over-the-top, wet-her-pants psyched Summer would be if Zac Trask and Gina Gerard showed up at her dorky little birthday bash.

"Better not alert the paparazzi on that one," Zara told Summer. "They've both made plans to be in other countries to avoid your party."

"What?" Summer's smile faltered. Zara could almost see the little wheels in the girl's head turning as she tried to figure out whether Zara was joking.

Even though Summer was getting on her nerves as usual, Zara felt a flash of guilt. A tiny one, anyway.

"Kidding. Duh," she said, rolling her eyes. "But yeah, they'll both be out of town then."

"Oh." Summer giggled. "Good one, Zara! You're coming though, right? I mean, you'll be at the show already, so obviously you'll come. Right?"

Before Zara had to answer, there was a sudden shout from the other end of the barn. It sounded like Fitz.

"What's going on?" Zara wondered. "Hope the new race-horse didn't decide the wash stall looked like a starting gate."

"I know, right?" Summer wrinkled her nose. "What was Fitz thinking, bringing some scrawny half-trained thing like that into the barn?"

Not really the point, but Zara didn't bother explaining. "Let's go see what's up."

She headed down the aisle, not bothering to see if Summer was following. The wash stalls were located in the center block of the barn at the opposite end from the feed room. They consisted of several large, airy bays with drains in the floor and hoses on overhead booms.

At the moment only one of the stalls was occupied. Fitz's new Thoroughbred was watching with pricked ears as Fitz, Kate, and Tommi surrounded someone in the aisle just outside the stall. Zara's eyes widened when she saw who it was.

"Dani!" she blurted out in surprise. "Whoa, didn't think we'd see her around here so soon."

"No kidding," Summer said. Then she rushed forward, shoving Kate aside to grab Dani. "Oh wow, Dani! Welcome back!"

Dani grinned sheepishly, leaning on one crutch to awkwardly return Summer's hug. "Hi, Summer. I figured I'd better stop in and show you all I'm still alive," she joked. "I also want to visit Red and let him know it wasn't his fault and I still love him." When she noticed Zara behind Summer, she lifted one hand. "Hey, Zara," she added. "You totally missed my involuntary dismount yesterday."

"Yeah, I heard it was pretty spectacular." Zara stared at Dani's cast, which covered her left leg from just above her toes to just below the knee. "You okay?"

"She got a nine on the somersault from the Russian judge, but then completely blew the landing," Fitz said.

"Very funny." Dani stuck out her tongue at him.

"Don't listen to him. We're all glad to see you," Kate said softly. Shooting Dani a smile, she ducked under the cross-ties and started working on the horse's far side with a sweat scraper.

"So Marissa said you had to have surgery," Summer said to Dani.

"Yeah, that was fun." Dani grimaced. "But I guess it went okay. I'm not supposed to put any weight on it for a while, but the doctors say I should be okay in about six weeks."

"Six weeks? That's not too bad," Tommi said. "You could be back in the saddle in time for Harrisburg."

"I hope so." Dani leaned on her crutches. "Anyway, I'll probably need all six weeks to convince my parents that I'm not going to—"

"There you are!" a loud voice rang out, cutting her off.

A girl Zara had never seen before stomped toward them. She was about their age, with overprocessed reddish-brown hair and hoochie-mama cutoffs. The girl ignored Zara and the others, her angry gaze focused on the horse in the wash stall. She jabbed a finger at it.

"I can't believe you stole him right out from under me!" she yelled.

Kate took a step out of the stall, gripping her sweat scraper so hard her knuckles were white. "Nat!" she exclaimed.

ACKNOWLEDGMENTS

I would like to acknowledge the teachers at the Spence School and at New York University, especially Ms. Eisenberg, Ms. Jewett, and Mr. Dinwiddie, who might have never been impressed with my writing but never let me believe that or accept failure. You always gave me just as much attention as the best student in the class and tried your very best to make me think I was as good as them if I believed in myself. Without your hard work and determination I would not have had the skills or the confidence to help write this book. There are a few of my past teachers who would be shocked that I am an author, and deservedly so. I apologize for making your job more difficult and for never appreciating the opportunity I had to learn from you. My only advice to you and to any teacher is to never give up on even the laziest, most rebellious student in your class. They may never show you that they appreciate it but I can say from experience that they will eventually. To the teachers who did this for me, I thank you and will always remember you.

Georgina Bloomberg

Kathy Russel

GEORGINA BLOOMBERG is the younger daughter of New York City mayor Michael Bloomberg. An accomplished equestrian, Georgina is on the board of directors of the Equestrian Aid Foundation and is the founder of the charity The Rider's Closet, which collects used riding clothes for collegiate riding teams that are unable to afford them. She also sits on the board of the Bloomberg Sisters and Bloomberg Family foundations. Georgina is a graduate of New York University's Gallatin School of Individualized Study.

Georgina is donating a portion of her proceeds from this book to the ASPCA.

CATHERINE HAPKA has published many books for children and young adults, including several about horses. A lifelong horse lover, she rides several times per week and keeps three horses on her small farm in Chester County, Pennsylvania. In addition to writing and riding, she enjoys animals of all kinds, reading, gardening, music, and travel.